NURSE ON THE RIVIERA

Nurse on the Riviera

Jane Converse

THORNDIKE
CHIVERS

This Large Print edition is published by Thorndike Press, Waterville, Maine USA and by BBC Audiobooks Ltd, Bath, England.

Thorndike Press is an imprint of Thomson Gale, a part of The Thomson Corporation.

Thorndike is a trademark and used herein under license.

Copyright © 1968 by Jane Converse.

The moral right of the author has been asserted.

LIBRARY OF CONGRESS CATALOGING-IN-PUBLICATION DATA

Converse, Jane.
  Nurse on the Riviera / by Jane Converse.
    p. cm. — (Thorndike Press large print candlelight)
  ISBN 0-7862-9179-6 (alk. paper)
  1. Nurses — Fiction. 2. Riviera (France) — Fiction. 3. Large type books. I.
Title.
PS3553.O544N8894 2006
813'.54—dc22   2006028613

BRITISH LIBRARY CATALOGUING-IN-PUBLICATION DATA AVAILABLE

Published in 2006 in the U.S. by arrangement with
Maureen Moran Agency.
Published in 2007 in the U.K. by arrangement with the author.

U.S. Hardcover: ISBN 13: 978-0-7862-9179-3; ISBN 10: 0-7862-9179-6
U.K. Hardcover: 978 1 405 63982 8 (Chivers Large Print)
U.K. Softcover: 978 1 405 63983 5 (Camden Large Print)

Printed in the United States of America on permanent paper
10 9 8 7 6 5 4 3 2 1

NURSE ON THE RIVIERA

CHAPTER 1

Terry Crane turned her patient's wheelchair so that light from the broad window wall fell over the small stack of letters she had just handed to Richard Olner.

Mr. Olner had already disposed of the mail forwarded each morning from his office. These were personal messages, and Mr. Olner's thick fingers, still uncoordinated in spite of his phenomenal recovery from a cerebrovascular accident, fumbled anxiously at tearing open one of the envelopes.

"You can manage, can't you?" Terry asked.

She knew what the answer would be. "Yes, certainly . . . why not?"

During the months she had served as Mr. Olner's special duty nurse at Mercy Hospital, and in the three months since he had returned to his luxurious home on Long Island, the man had demonstrated the same rugged determination and independence that had made him president of his own multimillion dollar electronics firm at the age of forty-six.

Cut down by a severe stroke, with one side of his body completely paralyzed, and with aphasia virtually destroying his ability to express himself with words, the man had pulled himself up from helplessness by an overpowering will. Therapists who had worried about tiring the man with prolonged sessions were themselves worn out. Inch by inch, Richard Olner had regained the use of his limbs so that he was able to walk now. True, he still relied upon a cane for support, and he obeyed Dr. Lindley's orders to limit even that physical exertion, but his progress had been astounding. Even more amazing had been the dogged persistence with which Mr. Olner had regained his speech. You helped a patient like this most by not offering to help him at all.

Terry looked around for a way to busy herself, letting Mr. Olner concentrate on his mail. There was little to do; Carl and Irene Washburn, with the help of a cleaning woman, took care of every household problem, leaving Terry with no responsibilities but the minor needs of her increasingly independent patient. Yet she felt obligated to stay in the room Mr. Olner called his study. Terry gazed out at the park-like grounds beyond the window wall. The lawn had not yet lost its drab winter-brown color, but the snow had dwindled to occasional gray clumps at the edge of the rose beds and under the stark leafless trees. It was a dismal scene, untouched by the forthcoming promise of spring.

Still, there was the certainty that in another month spring would come. The grass would flaunt its resurrected green freshness, the trees would burst with new life. There was always that firmly grounded hope. Her own dream was based on a flimsier faith. In two years, although Terry had been Dr. Lindley's choice as a private nurse for at least nine patients, he had never looked upon her as anything more than one unit in a medical package. An important unit (Bill Lindley was quick to recognize the value of a dedicated nurse), but no more than that.

Was it true that the doctor was still mourning the girl he would have been married to now, except for an ironic accident? He never spoke of it; in fact, he never revealed anything about himself. But it was known that he had lost the one love in his life in an automobile crash — a tragedy that had occurred while the girl was on her way to their wedding rehearsal. A sensitive man wouldn't recover easily from so traumatic a blow. Yet time softened the most agonizing grief, and life went on for the living. Bill Lindley was only in his early thirties. Was he really disinterested in women, replacing romance with a fierce dedication to his work? Or, more likely, was it that Terry held no charms for him — no personal interest at all? This latter possibility, though logical, was too painful to face. When you were this completely in love with a man, accepting hopelessness was . . . like looking out upon that dreary landscape and believing that April would never come.

Terry's melancholy introspection ended as her employer tossed his mail to a table at his side. "Well, at least two of my favorite people . . . aren't going to desert me," he said. "My son says he can't wait to get on the boat, and Wanda . . ." (Mr. Olner indulged himself in a fond chuckle) ". . . my baby wants . . . an addition to her allowance . . . so's she can start buying . . . a travel wardrobe."

There was a pleased glow to the man's already rose-tinged complexion, Terry noticed. Behind his dark-rimmed glasses, Richard Olner's eyes, ordinarily as colorless as his straight, wispy hair, sparkled now with an enthusiastic light, the shade of a gray-green sea. When he was happy about some-

10

thing, Terry had noticed, he seemed to have less difficulty in finding the words for expression. "Both my kids . . . anxious to come along on this . . . vacation trip. You could make it . . . perfect, Terry. Change your mind?"

Terry shook her head. "I appreciate your wanting me along, but . . ."

"Why shouldn't you come?" Richard Olner managed to shrug his massive shoulders, indicating that Terry's refusal was beyond his comprehension. "You don't have any . . . obligations here. The work won't be . . . any rougher than it's been. Less. I'm bound to . . . pick up strength. But . . . even with Carl and Irene around . . . I'll still need a nurse. Why are you . . . turning me down?"

Terry faked a careless laugh. "Maybe because I've heard that the French Riviera is an awful place. All those horrible beaches . . ."

"Seriously, Terry." Richard Olner's disappointment added an unaccustomed whining tone to his voice. The pleading sound didn't match the leonine strength of his features — the head that seemed too large for his recently wasted body, the firm jaw, and thick, barely visible neck that conveyed a sense of tremendous physical power. "You were the one who . . . backed up Doc Lindley. Remember? When he . . . said I won't be able to . . . separate myself from my . . . business as long as I'm here. Right along with my . . . doctor . . . my best friend . . . you said it was high time I started . . . relaxing . . . living, for a . . . change."

"It's true," Terry acknowledged. "You don't have to be at your office to absorb all the headaches of your firm. You do that right here. Next thing you know, you'll be right back at your desk, wearing yourself out."

"No, no . . . let's say I've . . . bought your bill of goods. I have. I'm not . . . indispensable. While I was . . . flat on my back in the hospital, the place ran right along . . . without me." Richard Olner flashed one of his quick, humorless smiles. "I'm not going to . . . starve to death if I start enjoying my . . . kids and my . . . friends."

There was a faint suggestion of regret in the man's speech now. Perhaps he was blaming his consuming interest in financial success for the breakup of two marriages and for his separation from the two grown children whose letters he had just read with so much pleasure. "I'm actually looking forward to a . . . long rest on the French Riviera. With my kids around, at least until September, I'll get to . . . make up for some of the . . . fun I've missed. Takes a major

12

shake-up like a . . . stroke . . . to teach a man what's . . . important."

It had taken a great deal of strong persuasion from Dr. Lindley, too, but Terry decided to let her patient think the European vacation was his own idea. "I've seen this happen often, usually with patients who've had an exceptionally close call. Suddenly they want to do all the things they've missed in life."

"It's like getting a second chance," Mr. Olner agreed. "Understand, I . . . if it meant giving up all the . . . material things I've accumulated . . . I doubt that I'd be . . . making any change. All that's happened is . . . I've discovered my business is . . . so well organized . . . it's going to go on making money whether I'm . . . there or not."

Terry smiled at the frank admission. "That's a good beginning, Mr. Olner. Being completely honest."

"Well, I didn't want you to think I'm . . . going to shave my head and . . . go live on rice in a . . . Tiger . . . Tibet . . . monk . . ."

Terry waited patiently, confident that he would overcome the difficulty with words that still plagued him occasionally.

". . . live in a Tibetan monastery," Mr. Olner finished resolutely. "We're leasing a beautiful villa. Should have nothing but fun." He paused, his expression surprisingly pained. "You're sure . . . you won't change your mind, Terry? I don't want to . . . pry into your personal life, but it . . . seems to me . . ."

". . . that you've offered me a glorious opportunity?" Terry poured a glassful of orange juice from a pitcher Irene had brought in with the morning mail. "I'd have to be crazy to argue that point. What's more, I'll probably kick myself one of these days for passing up a fabulous deal."

"But you won't come along?"

Terry shook her head. "I'm sorry."

There was a brief silence, during which Richard Olner was served his mid-morning fruit juice, drinking it down automatically and apparently without tasting it. The ideal patient, Terry thought. Determined to get well, and never questioning his doctor's orders. Cooperative patient, above-average salary, lovely living quarters, and now the opportunity to travel to one of the most glamorous areas of the world. What excuse could be offered, especially when Mr. Olner had already been told that Terry had no relatives, no personal commitments in New York?

When the silence became embarrassing, Terry blurted out the first explanation that

14

popped into her mind. "I've signed up for some summer courses. In . . . nursing administration."

"Is that what you want to do?" Richard Olner asked. He seemed to believe the story, accepting it glumly. "You want to . . . be a supervisor, or whatever?"

Terry forced another laugh. "You ought to approve that, Mr. Olner. Aren't you the one who says people who have what it takes shouldn't be contented with anything but the top job?"

"Yes, I . . . probably did say that." A gloom had descended over the man in the wheelchair, and he reached over to retrieve two of the letters on the table at his side. He began rereading one of them intently, perhaps to remind himself that the important people in his life were interested in sharing his new life. After a few seconds, as Terry started out of the room with the juice tray, he said, "We'll have to . . . call the registry today . . . for a replacement. Can't expect a new nurse to . . . be ready to leave the country on . . . two weeks' notice."

"No, that wouldn't be fair," Terry said. "You've already waited longer than you should have, Mr. Olner."

She felt an uncomfortable twinge of guilt, as though she had rejected someone in dire need. It was a foolish reaction; this was a wealthy patient whose health was improving. He was headed for a long, carefree vacation with familiar servants to take care of his needs and two members of his own family to keep him company. Any nurse could take over the minor duties that remained. At most, Terry's illogical decision might mean a slight blow to Mr. Olner's ego; he had made a charitable offer, and the offer had been refused. "I'll make the call, if you want me to," she said. "Or would you rather have Dr. Lindley arrange for a new nurse?"

"Doesn't matter."

The reply came in a sulking monotone, and Terry was glad to escape from the room. In another minute she would have been tempted to tell Mr. Olner the truth: leaving the area would mean a prolonged separation from Dr. Lindley. In a year, she would probably lose touch with the man she loved. Staying here, she could count on being assigned to another of his patients. Of course, she would see him only occasionally; the meetings would be brief and impersonal, as they were now. But there would be at least the faint hope. . . .

Carl Washburn was fond of pointing out

that if the Olner kitchen had been one square foot smaller, and his wife one round inch wider Irene would not have been eligible for her job. Fortunately, there was ample room for Irene's two-hundred-and-eighty-odd pounds, a blessing for which Richard Olner had cause to be grateful.

Observing her no-nonsense management of the household, and the heavy-handed certainty with which she prepared the meals, no one would have guessed that this behemoth of a woman had at one time worn the spangled leotards of a ballerina, forming part of the beefy come-on for a carnival posing show. Carl, who had been the silver-tongued "talker" for the show, had evidently praised the then-chubby glamour girl so many times for the benefit of gawking farmhands that he had convinced himself; they had been married twenty-one years ago, and his love for his wife had increased proportionately with the span of time and the spread of Irene's waistline.

After a lengthy career of roadshows, operating penny-pitch and six-cat games, the couple had graduated to a circus cookhouse, during which time Irene's culinary talents had flowered. Tired of one-night stands and the smell of popcorn, they had deserted their more glamorous professions to answer Richard Olner's ad for a couple: MAN TO DRIVE AND DO ODD JOBS, WIFE TO COOK AND SUPERVISE OTHER HELP. MUST BE SOBER, HONEST, INDUSTRIOUS.

Honest and industrious they were, and if Irene's grocery account seemed a trifle lopsided in favor of "cooking sherry," Mr. Olner, who knew a good deal when he saw one, was disposed to ignore that trifling matter. The Washburns had been in his employ for seven years, and not one of the three parties involved could visualize any other arrangement.

In their later forties, Carl and Irene had an ageless quality; they could as easily have been twenty-five or sixty. Sandy-haired, wiry, and inclined toward flashy clothing reminiscent of his carnival days, Carl had a puckish, freckled face that was dominated by a pair of ridiculously round and baby-blue eyes. Irene's eyes, at least what was visible of them through the fleshy folds of her face, had none of her husband's wide, childish innocence. Dark and worldly-wise, they kept close watch over the Olner estate, the daily racing form, and Carl — though not always in that order.

They were both in the kitchen when Terry came in to return the orange-juice pitcher and glass, Carl slouched down in a plastic chair studying his *Turf Guide* and Irene at a tile counter, kneading bread-roll dough in preparation for lunch.

"Mr. O. read his mail?" Irene invited. She had a consuming curiosity about her employer's personal correspondence.

Terry set the tray down and poured herself a cup of coffee. "Yup."

"Got one letter from his daughter and one from his son." Irene's palms attacked the dough furiously, her upper arms quivering with the effort. "You ain't ever met them two, have you, honey?"

Terry admitted that she hadn't, adding that "Mr. O." had rarely mentioned his offspring by his second wife. "He seemed awfully pleased, though. I guess they've both accepted his invitation."

Without raising his eyes from his racing sheet, Carl groaned. "Well, you can't win 'em all, Irene."

Irene ignored her husband, a fact so commonplace that it was barely worthy of notice. "I was feelin' sorry fer you, Terry. Missin' out on all the fun. But, I tell you . . ." Irene paused to shake her melon-shaped head dolefully. Her frizzed, bowl-cut coiffure, currently dyed a shade that hovered between copper and magenta, flopped from side to side in rhythmic assent. ". . . now I got an idea you won't be missin' nothin' but a lotta headaches. I sure like Mr. O., but them two brats . . ."

"They was here two summers ago," Carl muttered.

"Not at the same time," Irene added. "First, Wanda — and then Junior. What'd he call himself, sweetie? Tick?"

"Yeah. Tick." Carl tossed aside his daily inspirational reading matter and motioned for Terry to take a place at the kitchen table opposite him. "See, his name is Richard, but instead of they call the kid Dick or Rick, they call him Tick. You know what a tick is, sugar? A thing what gets under your skin."

"Boy, they got that one pegged right," Irene said. "Time he got on the plane and went home to his ma in Los Angeles, I was gettin' ready to put roach powder in his oatmeal."

"The girl was kinda cute," Carl ventured. A murderous glance from Irene tempered his opinion. "In a disgustin' kinda way." His childish face brightened with sudden animation. "So they're comin' along. We won't see much of 'em and it'll make Mr. O. happy, what the heck. You oughta join the pack, Terry. Get to eat snails, like them Frenchies do. Lotsa laughs. Listen, you

20

know what Irene bought herself? A new bathin' suit. No kiddin'. Custom tailored by the New York Tent an' Awning Company."

Irene sighed. "Ain't he a riot? Tell me if he ain't a scream?"

Carl released one of his boisterous laughs. His thumb projected the huge plastic badge pinned to the lapel of his unchauffeurlike checked sports jacket. He changed the "snappy sayings" badges daily, and today's read: I'M A CARD, KIDDO.

Terry sipped at her coffee, maintaining her usual neutrality in the affectionate hostilities.

Irene had started shaping the glob of dough into cloverleaf rolls, using enough energy to build a battleship. "A lotta chance I'll have to sun myself on them Rivee-ara beaches, the way the mob keeps growin'. I'll be cookin' my head off, that's what I'll be doin'." In a tone suggesting that she was revealing a deep philosophy, Irene said, "See, when it's somebody I like, fer them I like cookin'. Take Mr. O. Him, I knock myself out. You . . ." she nodded at Terry. ". . . you, I feel the same. Carl, I got no choice. Wanda an' Tick, I wouldn't even wanna boil snails for them two brats."

"Who else?" Carl demanded.

"Well, there's gonna be another nurse.

21

Her, I dunno. Maybe she'll be nice, like Terry, maybe I'll hate her guts. On her I got my mind open. Doc Lindley, that's somethin' else. Him, I like. See what I mean? Certain people, I go outta my way. Creeps, I resent it if they want a hunka toast. Take that Wanda now . . ."

"Dr. Lindley?" Terry barely sounded the name.

"I was talkin' about Mr. O.'s daughter," Irene snapped.

"No, but you said . . . Dr. Lindley. He isn't going . . ."

"Yeah, he's going," Carl said. "Didn't the boss tell you? Maybe Mr. O. don't know it yet."

Dumbfounded, Terry could only look inquiringly from one of the ex-carnies to the other.

Carl yawned. "Yeah, remember when the doc was here yesterday, he came into the kitchen after he saw Mr. O.?"

"He came for a slice of my lemon meringue pie," Irene pointed out. "Doc Lindley says I make the best . . ."

"Anyways, he said Mr. O.'s been tryin' to talk him into a vacation ever since they know each other, way back before the doc even was a out-tern or in-tern, or whatever they call them half-baked medics. All this

22

time, Lindley's never had a break. So, guess what? He's still sayin' no, he can't get away. And guess who talks him into it? Loud-mouth, over there. Fatty gave him a lotta lip about . . . what does he wanna do, kill himself workin', like Mr. O. did, an' then wind up flat on his back?"

Irene was undisturbed by the unflattering references to her figure or her "lip." Instead, she accepted Carl's explanation as highly complimentary. "Doc listens to me. He promised me he was gonna get these two other doctors to take over his patients. I'm surprised he ain't called Mr. O. to tell him yet, he's comin' to the Rivee-ara with us."

"All except twerpy Terry, here," Carl said.

"I didn't mention nothin' about Terry," Irene said. "For all the doc knows she's goin', too. Unless you or Mr. O. already asked him to find another nurse?"

"We didn't," Terry said. Her coffee cup had started shaking in her hands. "We didn't, and . . . we aren't going to."

CHAPTER 2

Richard Olner's determination that his "family safari" should be as prolonged and enjoyable as possible, precluded flying to France. Instead, Terry's happily received decision to join the party found her gathering together a modest shipboard wardrobe. Three weeks later, amid a flurry of serpentine ribbons, tooting of steam whistles, and waving crowds, the Atlantic crossing — and the dream — began.

Perhaps she had dwelled too long on the dream — visualized and expected too much. Less than a day out at sea, the excitement of departure had faded, and the thrill of exploring a luxurious floating palace had been replaced by a depressingly dull routine.

Mr. Olner, who had insisted before the arrival of his son and daughter that Terry refer to him as "Richard," apologized for the situation in his beautifully appointed stateroom. "I'm terribly sorry about you being stuck here with me, Terry. If you'd rather go up to dinner with the others . . ."

"And leave you here alone? I'm here as your nurse, remember?" Terry's voice carried more conviction than she felt inwardly.

"You're very sweet," Richard said. "Truth is, Bill Lindley's right about my getting overtired . . . overstimulated. We'll make up for the lost time when I'm a little stronger. No point in pushing too fast."

Terry agreed. During the day, the chill Atlantic winds made even a wheelchair promenade on the deck too uncomfortable for her patient. The dining room, the cocktail lounges, and the innumerable private parties that seemed to erupt after momentary conversations with strangers, placed too great a strain on a man who had spent the past few months following a sensible regimen of quiet and calm. "Dr. Lindley's absolutely right. And, really, I don't mind having dinner here with you. I don't . . ." Terry hesitated. "I don't really care for crowds."

Why disturb Richard with her uncomfortable sensation of being neither a vacationing guest nor a part of the help? While Richard's offspring saturated themselves in all the pleasures available to first-class passengers, Bill Lindley seemed to be recouping all the lost hours when he had denied himself anything that resembled fun. And while Carl and Irene — traveling tourist class and completely free of their normal chores — plunged into a manic social whirl, Terry felt herself excluded from everything but her job, from everyone except the congenial millionaire who was making this "dream trip" possible.

Dejected, but determined not to let her employer know it — after all, this was a job — Terry was trying to concentrate on a game of Scrabble when someone knocked on the door. She leaped up eagerly, glad of any interruption. "That'll be our steward with the dinner trays."

She opened the door, instead, on a resplendently attired trio; Dr. Lindley and Tick Olner, penguinlike in black-and-white dinner clothes, and Wanda, petite in a simply cut dinner dress of blue and silver brocade. With her auburn hair cut short in a shaggy, ultrachic coiffure, Richard's daughter looked considerably older than her eighteen years. Except for ludicrously long fingernails — attempt at sophistication — and a pale, luminous lipstick that gave her elfin face a somewhat freakish appearance, Wanda Olner presented a dazzling picture. She swept past Terry to place an arm around her father's shoulder. "Sure you don't feel up to having dinner with us, Daddy?"

Terry stood near the door, feeling awkwardly like the family maid as the two men filed into the room. Dr. Lindley nodded and smiled at her pleasantly. Tick Olner, laboring under the delusion that he was irresistible to women, favored her with what he undoubtedly considered a sexy stare; it resembled what it was — the smirk of a callow fop.

Not to be outdone by his sister in fawning over their father, Tick said, "Tell you what, Pops. I'll stay here with you. How's that?"

"No, you kids run along," Richard said. "I'll be fine with Terry."

It seemed to Terry that the very mention of her name sparked a flashing hostility in Wanda. "I'm sure you will," the girl said. "I just know she'd rather stay down here with you."

His daughter's caustic tone was lost on Richard. "Yes, we get along rather well, don't we, Terry?"

"June and December," Tick muttered under his breath. It was not the first time he had referred to the difference between his father's age and Terry's. He was an elongated and considerably less likable version of the man whose name he bore.

Though, like Wanda's, his eyes were of a peculiar hazel shade that had undoubtedly been inherited from their mother, Tick Olner had Richard's seemingly colorless hair and eyelashes. A thin wisp of a moustache, barely visible in the softly lighted compartment, quivered as he added aloud, "I guess any guy under thirty doesn't have a chance with young chicks anymore. They seem to have opened the season on . . ."

"Shut up, Tick." Wanda accompanied her warning with a hate-filled glare. Her brother responded by smiling a knowing, contemptuous smile. If their shared attitude toward Terry was patronizing and suspicious, there was also no love lost between them.

Bill Lindley, who had not moved from the closed door, glanced at his watch. "I wanted to talk to your dad for a few minutes before dinner," he said.

"Is that our cue to leave?" Tick asked. He was toying with a polished black cigarette holder, doing his best to look world-weary and bored.

Wanda gave a tinkling laugh that was no more genuine than her sweeping black eyelashes. "He's not getting rid of me that easily. I don't mind scooting now, but we're sitting at the same table tonight, Bill. And you promised we'd wear a hole in the ballroom floor afterward."

"I'll . . . meet you in the dining room," the doctor said. He shot Richard a look that implied he was being indulgent with his friend's less-than-grown-up youngster, even permitting the child a first-name familiarity.

He waited until Wanda and Tick were out of the room before explaining to Richard, "You wanted me to keep an eye on Wanda, but it seems to be working the other way around. She's not letting me out of her sight."

"Not a crush, I hope." Richard grinned. "She'll get over it. Meet some nice young college kid and forget you exist, old man."

"You make me sound like a geriatrics case," Dr. Lindley said. "Actually, I was looking forward to having dinner with a very interesting woman . . . a psychologist from Chicago. If Wanda comes back to report that I was beastly toward her, bear in mind that the ballroom bit was her own idea."

"Kids get spoiled," Richard said gravely. "When they have two parents competing for their affections, they learn to play one against the other. Then they get the idea they can manage anybody — get anything they want." He winked at Terry. "They're still good kids. Notice the way they take time to . . . run down here? With all the fun things they've got to do, they . . . still care how the old man's doing."

"You aren't an old man," Terry said. She said it because she knew Richard had invited the assurance. Yet she wondered if perhaps he wasn't whistling in the dark when he pointed out his children's consideration for him. Actually, Tick and Wanda hadn't spared him more than fleeting visits. Apart from obvious flattery, they seemed to have little to say to him, and the concern they showed was so patently insincere that anyone as shrewd as Richard should have been able to see through it; they were "managing" him to get what they wanted.

Dr. Lindley's visit was a routine affair that had little to do with the state of Richard's health. The pair were old friends, and their conversation covered a wide span of casual topics — from none of which was Terry excluded. Yet she longed to run from the room, suddenly finding the sight of the man she loved unbearably painful.

Tall, lean, strangely muscular and tan considering his all-work-and-no-play existence, Bill Lindley exuded an attraction from which other women were probably not immune. He had dark serious eyes that looked directly at the person he was addressing, and the deep quiet resonance of his voice

30

had a magnetism of its own. Terry was seeing him through the eyes of other women now: the strong, sharply delineated features, his sensitive yet oddly sensuous mouth, the broad forehead outlined by neatly clipped, dark-brown hair. He managed to look self-assured without a trace of smugness, compassionate without a suggestion of weakness.

His virile good looks might appeal to a shallow little headhunter like Wanda, but his keen intelligence would attract more discerning women; the fastidious women Terry had seen in the dining room on the first night at sea. There were always romance-hungry women who moved in the upper social strata as easily as Bill Lindley moved. He had just mentioned one. And after years of emotional deprivation, he was as likely to resist these attractions as a man lost on the Sahara was likely to by-pass an oasis.

Terry forced herself to stay and to listen to the genial small talk. It seemed an eternity before Bill Lindley said goodnight and headed for his rendezvous with Wanda Olner.

Another hour dragged by, during which their dinner trays were brought in and then removed, and then Richard nodded at the

Scrabble board and said, "Shall we finish our game?"

In the quiet of the exquisitely decorated cabin, with her imagination following her heart to the music, the laughter, the promise of romance on the decks above, Terry felt as though the wishful game she had been playing was already finished.

Terry's disillusionment, as Bill Lindley was swallowed up in an unceasing round of shipboard parties, might have been bearable without added irritations from her employer's offspring.

Tick and Wanda made a deliberate effort to be civil toward her in their father's presence, but they rarely passed up an opportunity to emphasize the social and economic difference between Terry and the Olner clan. Though they had spent the better part of their lives separated from their father, they behaved as though they were a devoted family, "democratic" toward menial outsiders, but determined not to accept such strangers into their inner circle. And their unsubtle references to the difference between Richard Olner's age and Terry's were like a constantly recurring theme.

At first, Terry ignored their sniping, attributing it to bad manners and letting it go at that. But, gradually, it became apparent that she was a peculiarly personal target; there seemed to be some definite purpose in their hostility. It became obvious the day before their ship was due to dock at Marseilles.

At his doctor's invitation, and with Terry's assistance, Richard had ventured to one of the lounges for a game of chess. Feeling superfluous, Terry left her patient with his doctor friend. She was on her way to her own quarters, wondering how best to spend the unexpected hour of leisure, when she met Tick Olner in one of the narrow passages connecting the first-class compartments. Tick had evidently gone to visit his father and found the door locked.

He didn't bother to greet her. "Where's my dad?" he asked. As usual, his eyes looked Terry over as though she were merchandise he was considering for purchase.

Terry explained the situation, then moved forward to find the obnoxious young man blocking her way. His expression now was one of arrogance and uncomfortably personal interest.

"In a hurry?" Tick asked lazily.

"I'd like to get to my room, if you don't mind." Terry's firmness was betrayed by the quaver of anger in her voice.

Tick's leering expression hardened and then turned into a superior smirk. "I left my cigarette lighter in my dad's room. I imagine you have the key?"

Terry nodded, looking past the obstacle in her way. "I'll let you into the compartment if . . ."

"Never mind. Just get my lighter and bring it up to the Nautilus Bar." Tick stepped aside and brushed past Terry, on his way to the nearest stairwell.

For a split second, the deliberate attempt at humiliation left Terry speechless with resentment. Then, before Tick Olner had gone more than a few steps, Terry said, "If I were you, I wouldn't hold my breath waiting for it, Junior. I don't happen to be your private maid."

"You're supposed to be working for . . ."

"Your *father*," Terry reminded him. "As an R.N., not as a lackey. And if you want to report me to your dad for insubordination, by all means go right ahead."

She didn't turn back to see Tick's reaction, but hearing him stomp up the metal steps she was able to imagine his fury. Ten minutes later, in the less stilted atmosphere of a small lounge on the tourist-class deck, Terry sipped iced tea, watched Carl and Irene Washburn sip at something stronger, and recounted the incident with Tick Olner.

"That's tellin' 'im," Carl exclaimed when Terry had finished her story. "Exactly what that smart punk needs." Carl looked resplendent in a new red jacket, complete with a gold-embroidered crown on its pocket. It had been purchased on board with winnings from the ship's pool, in which passengers placed bets on the number of knots they traveled each day. "Listen, Irene and me, we don't even let little Junior treat us like servants. And that's what we're supposed to be."

Irene nodded her approval. A fabulous cuisine, with unlimited between-meal buffets and snacks, had done nothing to reduce her avoirdupois, but she was reveling in the experience. "Carlie, if you see the 'steward,' see can you get him to get us somethin' to nibble. Like them little cocktail meat balls we had yesterday." Having taken care of her own most pressing problem, Irene returned her attention to Terry's. "Not that them two kids of Mr. O.'s need any rehearsing in how to be repulsive, understand. But five gets you ten they got a little coachin' from their ma before they left home."

Terry frowned. "I don't get it."

"Why do you think you're poison to Junior an' his sister?" Irene demanded.

Terry shrugged. "I don't know." A sudden ludicrous thought struck her and she grinned. "Maybe they think I have matrimonial designs on their father."

Irene's round face remained impassive. "You bet your sweet life they do, honey. They want their old man to get married again like I wanna gain twenty pounds." Before her husband could remind her that she had hardly been observing a starvation diet, Irene threw him a warning glance. "No remarks from you, Hotshot. What I mean is, they know if there's gonna be a new Mrs. O., it'll probably be bye-bye big bundle. Know what I mean? They could count on some loot when their dad cashes in his chips, but if there's a young wife around, they ain't about to get nowheres near all of it."

Carl nodded as though his wife had spoken one of life's deepest truths. "So you're wonderin' why you ain't popular with them two . . ."

"But that's ridiculous!" Terry interrupted. "It's the most asinine idea in the world!"

Irene arched her brows. "Yeah?"

"You know it's the furthest thing from my mind. Mr. Olner's almost old enough to be my father." Terry thought for a moment. "Almost, nothing! I'm exactly the same age

36

as Tick. He's twenty-four, right? Okay, Mr. Olner's . . ."

". . . got eyes," Irene said flatly. "He married two different losers, and he ain't about to get tied up with another money-happy dame. But he ain't about to be *dis*interested in one that's pretty, that's been real good about helpin' him get well, that's . . ."

"That's ridiculous!" Terry exclaimed. "He hasn't shown the faintest signs of personal interest in me, except as a nurse and . . . as a friend."

"He won't, either, until he's able to get around like he used to," Carl said. "He wouldn't take the chance of bein' turned down, and he wouldn't want you feelin' sorry for him, either. I know the boss. He's got a lotta pride, an' when he wants somethin', he's patient until the time is right. He even told me . . . that's how he operates his business."

"And he liked to of died when it looked like you weren't comin' along on this trip," Irene remembered. "He kept needlin' me to talk you into it."

In spite of the Washburns' conviction, Terry refused to accept the possibility of any romantic interest on Richard Olner's part. "He's gotten used to me as a nurse," she argued. But there was no arguing the other possibility: that Tick and Wanda had probably pegged her as a fortune hunter. She sighed. "I don't suppose it would do any good to drop the word that I don't have any ideas about becoming Mrs. Olner."

Carl drained his glass. "Nah. Those kids are such con artists, themselves, you'd only convince them you were puttin' on an act. Best thing is, ignore 'em. If they get too salty, tell Mr. O. He'll put 'em in their place."

"And that'll really convince them," Terry said.

There was a glum silence, indicating agreement. Irene had spotted a steward, and was frantically waving at him. Finally, Carl said, "Once we get settled, they'll be out tearin' around. You won't hardly see the brats."

There was a better idea, Terry thought. Quit the job and take the first plane back home.

It was an idea that would free her of feeling like a cross between a ruthless gold digger and a neglected Cinderella. Yet, half an hour later, as Terry returned to the upper deck lounge to see if her patient was ready to return to his rooms, she knew that the plane would leave without her. She could take considerably more annoyance from

Richard Olner's son and daughter, as long as her heart started beating faster, as it did now, at the thought of merely seeing Bill Lindley once more.

CHAPTER 3

Richard Olner had given his broker carte blanche in leasing a villa on the Cote d' Azur. He could not have placed his trust in better hands.

A few hours' drive south from Marseilles, the building dominated a high promontory overlooking the sparkling blue-and-white expanse of the Mediterranean. A massive structure of pink-hued stone that had apparently been sawed into uniform bricks, its many slate-shingled, steeply slanted rooflines suggested that the architect favored Norman design; the few other imposing houses in the area were covered with white tiles. At one end of the broad rectangle, the builder had indulged himself in a circular, peaked tower. The façade here, like the rest of the building, was interrupted by high, extremely narrow, latticed windows.

Although the villa jutted skyward two tall stories high and seemed to teeter near the edge of a three-hundred-foot cliff, it was blended into the landscape by slightly less towering palms and a surrounding wall of pink stone over which red and purple bougainvillea had been splashed in colorful abandon.

Twin rows of twisted olive trees lined the road that led from the coastal highway to the walled rear gardens, the latter a riotous floral display as fragrant as the nearby perfume center of Grasse.

From the ledge and from the windows of the upper story, one could also glimpse, far below and to the south, a ribbon of white sandy beach dotted with tiny fishing boats. Beyond the dilapidated but picturesque quay and a weather-beaten, toylike lighthouse, nestled the humble cottages that comprised St. Juste.

The village had, thus far, escaped the inroads of dubious progress which were swiftly covering areas of the coastline with luxurious apartment complexes. Perhaps its miniature beach and lack of night life were St. Juste's temporary salvation. Its quaintness, its sun-drenched scenic beauty, were commonplace along the azure coast, and since it boasted no hotel worthy of the name, no gourmet restaurants and no gambling casino, the village held few attractions as a playground for the international jet set, nor even the less affluent tourists who scurried through on their way to Cannes, to Nice, to Monaco and, ultimately, the Italian Riviera.

"Actually, it just barely qualifies as a village," Bill Lindley said on the second day after the party had settled itself in the villa. He had found Terry gazing down at the storybook hamlet over a low protective wall that edged the cliff. A fresh offshore breeze rustled through the palm fronds; the sun intensified the blue-green brilliance of the sea. "I drove down this morning. It's a cluster of fishermen's cottages around a little square of a park. One grocery shop, two wine-cellars."

"It sounds lovely," Terry said.

The doctor laughed. "I didn't mean to belittle the place. It's beautiful, all right. What I meant was that I didn't find what I was looking for. Eventually, I did . . . there's a more substantial village, a few miles inland, called Roberval. Small clinic there, and a doctor who impressed me very favorably."

"A doctor?"

"Yes, a Dr. Armand Gautier. Trained in Paris and Vienna — hardly a provincial village medic. He's young, he's progressive,

42

and, among other assets, he speaks English."
Perhaps in answer to Terry's puzzled expression, Dr. Lindley explained, "I'm only going to be here for a month, you know. Richard's planning to stay indefinitely. Before I leave, I want to be sure there's someone you can call in case of emergency. And to supervise Richard's general therapy."

Somehow, Terry hadn't thought about the difference in their schedules. Of *course* Bill Lindley couldn't leave his practice for more than a short period! After that, she would find herself alone again, separated from even brief, impersonal contacts like these. Terry swallowed her disappointment. "It's thoughtful of you to . . . plan for your replacement."

"You make it sound so gloomy. I've just arrived, and here I'm practically on my way back to the office. While I'm here, though, I'm going to make the most of it." Dr. Lindley made a wry face. "On my own, if I can convince Wanda that I don't need an adolescent tour-guide." He glanced over his shoulder in a facetious gesture. "I'm hiding now, as a matter of fact."

Terry searched for a comment that would keep her from getting further involved with a girl who already detested her. "She's . . . quite persistent."

"Like her father, when he decides he wants something," the doctor said. "I think she'd have preferred staying in Nice or Cannes. As she puts it, 'where the action is.' Her brother's already announced that he doesn't intend to waste too much time around here. That should be pleasant news for you, Terry."

He had noticed, then, that the Olner offspring weren't Terry's idea of pleasant company. "I'm not going to let them bother me," she said.

"You can't very well, under the circumstances," Dr. Lindley said. "I'm afraid they're a part of your package deal."

For no reason that Terry could fathom, there was a cutting edge of sarcasm in Bill Lindley's tone. Although he claimed he was avoiding Wanda, he turned toward the house suddenly, as if he had remembered a pressing appointment. "Richard still napping?" he asked.

"Yes, I . . . talked him into taking a rest," Terry said. "The trip tired him, I think. More than he's willing to admit."

"Typical." The doctor took several steps toward the front terrace, then hesitated. "I've asked Dr. Gautier to stop in and get acquainted later today. He thought he'd get up here after dinner tonight. Will you be free then?"

"I'm sure I will," Terry said. She was left with the bitter reminder that she would, indeed, be free, because there was no place for her to go unescorted. Except for her patient and the Washburns, none of whom were likely to be going anywhere tonight, she was completely alone.

Determined not to feel sorry for herself, Terry searched for distractions. She began in the rose garden, practicing her tourists' phrase-book French on an elderly gardener who was also, it seemed, "a part of the package deal." At any rate, like the cook and maids who were the new bane of Irene Washburn's existence, the wizened old man appeared to belong to the villa, exhibiting only the vaguest interest in the new occupants. His indifferent manner suggested that renters came and renters went, but the old house had been standing for uncounted years, and the roses would bloom and need spraying when the current crop of strangers had gone back to wherever they belonged.

Terry's *"Bonjour, Jean-Pierre"* elicited a disinterested grunt. Her more daring, *"Comment allez-vous?"* brought forth a grudging, *"Pas mal,"* without an interruption in his work or an inquiry about the state in which

Terry found herself.

Discouraged with her attempt at Gallic repartee, Terry chatted for a few minutes with Carl, who had found himself in charge of a veritable fleet of rented Peugeots, and, with nothing better to do, was inside the garage giving the foreign cars a wary inspection. He, too, was hiding from someone, he said. "Irene's so mad at that babe in the kitchen she ain't fit to be around," Carl complained. "Go see if you can bring her blood pressure down a couple notches, honey."

Terry decided to occupy another few minutes in the kitchen. What she encountered was not only the proverbial beehive of activity, but a hornet's nest of hostile femininity as well.

At one end of the spacious tiled room, a tiny, birdlike woman, wearing a crisply starched white uniform not unlike Terry's, was busily concocting what appeared to be enough food for a regiment. Surrounded by cheeses, herbs, a bowlful of eggs, several opened bottles of wine and an assortment of bewildering culinary gadgets, the woman was attacking her project as though the fate of the solar system hinged upon the results.

The woman's speed indicated competition; the way she banged pots and bowls

46

against the tiled counter indicated anger. Her thin face was an impassive mask, but her dark eyes blazed with righteous contempt. Like the gardener, she evidently considered herself a fixture, and there was no doubt that she didn't intend to be displaced by three hundred pounds of American fury.

Irene had stationed herself near the mammoth stove. If her belligerent stance meant anything, the war of the cooks would be fought out on that illustrious battlefield. Shaking with frustration, she looked like a cross between a Valkyrie and a gelatin salad. "Listen, how do I get it across to this dame that I do the cookin'?" she cried. "Tell her I'm Mr. O.'s personal cook. Me. Not her. *Me.*"

Terry didn't risk showing her amusement. "Have you tried to explain that to her?"

"Yeah, sure. In English. She awready looks at me like I'm some kinda nut."

"Try French," Terry suggested.

Irene gave her a scathing look. "You think I didn't try that? Carl brings me one of them trans-a-lation books, but it don't say nothin' in there about what happens when the boss rents a house that awready comes with hot an' cold runnin' cooks. All I found out how to say was 'I want a room with a

47

private bath.' " Irene glared in the direction of the clanging cutlery. "That wouldn't cut no ice with Tootsie-Belle over there."

Irene had additional sorrows. "She got the edge on me, I gotta say that. I don't even know how I'm gonna shop. It ain't like pickin' up the phone an' tellin' Herbie the butcher I wanna nice rib roast. Here I walk in some strange place, nobody knows what I'm talkin' about. You know what I found out? They got this crazy thing here, they sell the stuff by the kilo. Me, I don't know a kilo from a Pekinese pup. What am I supposed to do?"

"I'm sure Mr. Olner will straighten it all out when you explain the situation," Terry assured her. To soothe Irene's injured pride, she said, "I'm also sure he knows you're a better cook."

"That's what's killin' me," Irene muttered. "I ain't." Hastily, she added, "But don't get the idea I'm lettin' no foreign alien push me around. Soon as her highness gets through, I'm startin'."

"You mean we're going to have two dinners tonight?" It was impossible to keep a straight face now.

"You got it right, kiddo." Irene planted her ample backside firmly against the oven door. "And guess which one is gonna get served?"

She was still manning her battle station when Terry left the kitchen. Apparently Irene's adversary made a move toward the stove and was thwarted, for as Terry mounted the stairway, she heard a voice shrilling, *"Vous avez l'intention de rester ici? Sacré bleu! Vous vous rendez insupportable!"*

Whatever the resident cook was screaming, it seemed unlikely that Irene would be able to argue her down by requesting a room with a private bath.

CHAPTER 4

Although the rented villa had been built more than a century ago, it had been re-decorated and furnished by a nouveau-riche owner in the dying years of the nineteenth century.

Terry's upstairs bedroom, to her relief, had been touched by a lighter hand than the rest of the house; here the white and gold pieces, of an undetermined period, were slender, graceful, and not overly ornate. Shell-pink satin, now faded to a delicate warm beige tone, had been quilted to upholster the headboard and bedspread, then lavishly gathered to cover a curved canopy and dust ruffle. Stylized pink-to-mauve roses decorated the wallpaper. Its background (once undoubtedly white) had mellowed with age to a soft eggshell color, and if the pattern was disproportionately large, considering the room's Lilliputian petit-point chairs, the overall effect was not displeasing.

In the lower rooms, the decor might have been labeled Early Ostentatious, yet there was no questioning the workmanship that had gone into curvilinear, unsymmetrical, and elaborately carved mahogany bookcases, chiffoniers, commodes, desks, and ubiquitous footstools. A few pieces, including a serpentine-shaped table in the grand salon, might have been identified by a more discerning eye than Terry's, as genuine eighteenth-century creations; a rosewood Pleyel piano in the smaller reception room referred to as the *petit* salon was, if not a museum-quality antique, certainly a collector's item.

If there was an undecorated surface anywhere in the house, the omission escaped even careful inspection. There was no tabletop that was not profusely inlaid with floral designs in tulipwood and ivory, no chair leg that failed to terminate in leaf-scroll feet, intricately carved whorls, or shell designs. Gilt and lacquer wedded the brief Chinese influence on Louis XV furnishings with the fin de siècle vogue for Oriental rugs; the latter covered virtually every square inch of floor in the lower rooms.

Baroque styling reached its zenith in the dining room, where the newly affluent owner had indulged in an orgy of low-relief wall panels and dadoes (the wood almost metallic with thick coatings of gilt), heavy green brocade draperies, and massive chairs that had been scrolled, embellished with marquetry and upholstered in red velvet.

On the walls, a gold-framed portrait of somebody's grandmother-as-a-young-girl faced a grouping of grimmer relatives, immortalized in daguerrotypes, their dark tin likenesses matted with more red velvet, framed with more gilded curlicues. They vied for attention with pale pastoral scenes: shepherds, sheep, and impossible landscapes printed on wallpaper and set into the (again!) gold-brushed wall panels.

Bill Lindley, who had somehow found time to acquaint himself with French period furnishings, expressed the general feeling when he wondered aloud how anyone could assemble so many exquisite pieces and build from them a monument to bad taste.

Yet, while the Saucepan War raged in the kitchen, the dinner table was set with translucent Haviland china from Limoges, and, as Terry accompanied her patient into the dining room that evening, she was glad she had exchanged her uniform for a periwinkle-blue silk sheath that complemented her eyes, glad she had pinned her long black hair into a simple and sophisticated coiffure that called for glittering earrings. The setting, in spite of its daytime garishness, had a quiet elegance under candlelight. Wanda, she noticed, had chosen to wear an imported paisley sari-like affair that was a perfect showcase for her petite figure; to have worn anything but her best would have made Terry feel shabby.

Richard Olner reached the dining room with only the support of his cane maneuvering even the stairway unaided. With Terry beside him at the table, he grinned triumphantly at his doctor and at his son and daughter. "Give me a few more weeks," he said, "and I'll be creaming the rest of you on a tennis court."

There was polite laughter. Then, as the conversation drifted to the various activities the others expected to enjoy on the Riviera, a stoic young serving maid, properly formal in black with pleated white organdy accents, began serving a dinner that would have done justice to France's immortal chef, Carême.

"Escargots farcis," Tick said in a blase tone. He delighted in showing off his pathetic French and had a snobbish regard for himself as a gourmet. "When did that walrus . . . what's her name? Irene? When did

she graduate to stuffed snails?"

Terry couldn't resist telling about the incident in the kitchen, finishing with, "I have an idea Irene's finally met her match. She can browbeat anyone, from Carl on up, but that other woman is on firmer ground. After all, it's her country. And I guess she's been around so long that she considers the kitchen here hers, too."

Bill Lindley and Richard were amused; Wanda and Tick, on the contrary, exchanged supercilious glances.

Richard turned toward Terry. "I'm going to let you be the referee, dear. Irene likes you, and you're the most hopeful candidate in the family when it comes to communicating in French. Work it out so that everybody's happy."

"I think you overestimate me and underestimate the feud," Terry said. "Short of firing . . . I believe her name is Yvonne . . . and I don't think you'd want to do that. . . ."

"No, we'd be extremely unpopular here if we did that," Richard agreed. "Jenson . . ." (he referred to his broker) ". . . should have let me know this place was already staffed. But, then, I didn't tell him I was bringing the Washburns." Richard was thoughtful for a moment. "One solution might be giving Carl and Irene a real vacation. I won't be going anywhere for a few weeks, anyway, so there's no need for a chauffeur." He nodded at the others. "The rest of you would rather drive yourselves. What about that idea, Terry? Carl loves to gamble. Scoot them up to Nice or Monaco for a little fling?"

"Why, that's outrageous!" Tick cried out. He modified his statement quickly. "I don't mean to criticize you, Dad. The point is — when you start babying people in that class, they walk all over you. You're paying the Washburns to do a job, not to loaf around. All right, there was a mix-up and you have too many servants. First of all, I'd let them know I won't stand for any bickering. And then I'd get rid of one batch or the other."

"Get 'rid' of Carl and Irene?" Richard pronounced his words as though his son had just spoken the ultimate blasphemy.

Tick's face colored, and the pale, pencil-line moustache quivered slightly. "I know you have strong loyalties, Dad. In fact, that's . . . one of the characteristics I admire most in you, but . . . you've been through a lot. I can't see you getting emotionally upset because a couple of harpies can't get along in the kitchen."

"Tick's right," Wanda said. "It's nice to be democratic, but there's being reasonable,

55

too." Her eyes flicked momentarily in Terry's direction. "After all, when you start thinking of the help as part of the family — letting them make your decisions for you — you're asking for headaches."

Bolstered by his sister, Tick returned to his argument with renewed vigor. "Put your foot down, Dad. If it were my choice, I'd send the Washburns back to the carnival lot where they belong. Since you have some . . . sentimental attachment to them, I won't argue. Dump the local servants, and don't worry about something as nebulous as good will. You're paying for what you get, so who cares if the natives grumble a little?"

"You're too sweet, Daddy," Wanda said. "You really are. You forget that people who don't have anything are anxious to get what you've got. You let them get too familiar, instead of keeping them in their place."

Richard had been silent through this honeyed harangue. He obviously had no idea that while his son and daughter were discussing the Washburns they were actually referring to Terry. Furthermore, Richard's eagerness to win the affection of his children away from his wife was a considerable factor. He reveled in their flattery, eating up such carefully calculated phrases as "You're too sweet, Dad. . . . You let people take

56

advantage of you."

If Bill Lindley was aware of the attack on Terry, he politely excluded himself from it, and Terry suppressed her disgust with the young Olners by reminding herself that they didn't matter. Their hostility was based on a false assumption; she had no interest in Richard Olner except as a nurse who had helped him toward recovery. Before long, she would not have even that value to him. How would Wanda and Tick behave, she wondered, if they knew of her consuming love for another man seated at this table? What would be their reaction if the truth were known: that she had traveled to this distant country, was even willing to endure the humiliation of their subtle insults, because once or twice a day for the next month Dr. Lindley might exchange a few friendly words with her?

The reminder that what Tick and Wanda said didn't matter was not enough. Terry felt herself lapsing into a depression that was rooted in hopelessness. Why stay? Bill had changed the subject, and was now talking about his plans for himself — plans that were partially engineered by Wanda and in no way included a nurse who was "part of the help."

Discussion centered for a while around a

party, that night, at a nearby villa also occupied by American expatriates, a middle-aged couple from Texas whom Wanda had met on the beach that afternoon and from whom she had wangled an invitation. "Dull characters, actually," Wanda said, "but they know a lot of the right people in Cannes and Nice and Monaco. They know their way around Cap d'Antibes, and they know enough to steer us away from the places where all you meet are French store clerks on a scrimpy two week vacation. We need people like that if we're going to get in with the right crowd."

Wanda seemed torn between disappointment and relief when Bill Lindley begged off because he was expecting a visit from the local doctor. She was not enthusiastic about being escorted by her brother; clinging to the arm of a handsome and successful doctor would have enhanced her image with the "in people." Conversely, she appeared to resent leaving Terry alone with her father. It was funny, Terry thought; she'd almost invite me along just to forestall a romantic evening between her imaginary money-hunter and poor Richard!

When his "kids" had soared off to the party, although he wouldn't admit that he was tired, Richard Olner retired to his room. "I have some reports from my plant manager that I want to study," he explained. "When your local medic gets here, Bill, bring him up to the room. I'll be wide awake."

Twenty minutes later, when Terry looked in on him, Richard was peacefully asleep. Thrilled by the prospect, Terry refreshed her makeup, dabbed a drop of her favorite scent behind her ear, and made her way down the stairs to the *petit* salon.

Dr. Lindley was standing at the rosewood piano, desultorily picking out a one-fingered and unrecognizable melody. He stopped as Terry came into the room, crossing the Oriental rug to a plum-colored velvet sofa and sinking down. "Have you mediated in the kitchen yet?" he asked.

Terry sat down in a brocade-upholstered chair facing him. It was an effort to control her breathlessness and to appear casual. "No, I'm not up to that. It'll wait until morning." She was tired of the subject. *Steer the conversation to medical subjects,* her mind flashed. *Let him see how many interests we have in common. . . .*

"I imagine you run into these ticklish petty problems when you're trying to run a big household," the doctor was saying. His expression looked querulous. "One of the

59

sacrifices expected of the lady of the manor."

Terry managed a laugh. "If you mean I've been elected to do the dirty work, Doctor . . ."

"Bill," he corrected. "You heard Richard refer to all of us as family tonight." Once again there was an incomprehensible irony in his tone, but his smile was pleasant enough. "Or you can think of me as one of those soap opera characters . . . Old Doctor Bill. Friend of the family. Richard's poor but loyal old crony."

Terry laughed again at the pseudo-dramatic declaration, but she felt a vague uneasiness — as though Bill was only skimming the surface of what was on his mind. It was too absurd to assume that he had been influenced by Wanda. He wasn't foolish enough to think that Terry had any matrimonial traps set for Richard Olner. No, he was close enough to his patient to know better; he was being facetious because he couldn't think of anything seriously worth discussing with a mere nurse.

There was an awakward period of quiet before Terry seized on a remotely promising subject. "Tell me about the little clinic at Roberval, Bill. Is it strictly an outpatient facility, or does it serve as a hospital?"

Bill's face brightened. "Oh, they don't need colored lines painted on the floors to guide people to the right departments. It's small, but I'd guess there are fifteen . . . maybe as many as twenty beds. Not badly equipped, either, for a town that's too small to rate being on the map. I saw the X-ray room . . . last word in equipment. And Surgery. It's a far cry from what you'd find in New York, but then this isn't Paris. You have to compare it with Podunk, and offhand, I don't know of any American town of comparable size that could offer better emergency treatment."

He went on — and though Terry had asked the question, she gave only half an ear to the detailed answer. She let herself luxuriate in the mere sound of Bill's voice, noting his animation when he spoke about the subject closest to his heart, noting trivialities like the vivid pattern of the sport shirt he was wearing. He had worn the shirt with casual slacks to the dinner table in spite of the fact that the Olners had all made it a dress occasion.

Terry was accustomed to seeing the doctor in whites or in extremely conservative, dark business suits; since the beginning of this adventure he had blossomed out in colorful sports attire, perhaps a symbolic expression of his long-denied break from a grueling work schedule.

He was saying, "You'd find it interesting to visit the place, Terry. It may be a post-man's holiday sort of thing, visiting a hospital, but try to . . ." Bill cut off his sentence as one of the maids came into the room.

"Pardonnez-moi, m'sieu, mais le médecin est ici."

It was over. Whatever hope there had been of establishing a closer rapport with Bill evaporated as he got to his feet, crossing the salon to greet the new arrival. Terry found herself resenting the local doctor before she met him.

It was difficult, however, to resent Dr. Gautier for more than a fleeting moment. As Bill led the dapper young Frenchman into the room, after greeting him in the vestibule, Terry's annoyance with the intrusion melted under a barrage of Gallic charm.

Armand Gautier was barely a half inch taller than Terry; Bill towered over him. His wavy black hair had been brilliantined to a sparkle that matched his quick-flashing smile, and his eyes dominated his face like two ripe black plums. Within the brief course of their introduction, his rather fine features reflected a half dozen changes in mood, and Terry had the impression that this hypercharged man was capable of turning from deep seriousness to light flirtation to explosive laughter and then to a sudden, morbid gloom in the time it took most people to decide how they felt.

One thing became apparent seconds after the surprisingly youthful, nervously energetic local doctor made his entrance: no one could ever accuse him of not draining every instant of his life of everything it had to offer, for better or for worse.

Furthermore, the volatile and expressive doctor did not suppress his overwhelming curiosity about people. His inquiries were blunt, direct, and almost boyishly naïve. And inevitably, when Bill excused himself to go upstairs and tell Richard Olner that the doctor had arrived, the questions were directed to Terry in a strong but pleasant-sounding accent.

"You are the very private nurse to Monsieur Olnair, or not too much private? Perhaps you were also, how you say, sweetheart?" The dark eyes looked incisively into Terry's, half accusing, half admiring.

Terry couldn't help smiling at the frank inquisition, though from a less direct person she would have considered the questions presumptuous. "I'm Mr. Olner's nurse. Period. That's all."

Dr. Gautier accepted the answer hesitantly. "Not sweetheart?"

"Not sweetheart," Terry repeated firmly.

She had never before seen a more childishly bewildered expression on a face that otherwise indicated keen intelligence. In the next instant, Dr. Gautier seemed to be giving the matter grave thought, saying, "My English is not yet so superior. I make so often the mistake." Another second and he was jogging across the room, his bouncy steps and the excitable gesturing of his hands totally out of keeping with his immaculate and conservative attire. "Ah! Then you are the sweetheart of the so distinguish doctor, *oui? Certainement!* He did not make mention — but this arrangement, naturally suggests itself."

Regretfully, Terry assured him that this guess, too, was wrong.

Dr. Gautier shook his head uncomprehendingly, meanwhile letting his eyes give expert attention to Terry's dress. "A man would not dream you are a nurse! But, you Americans . . . *toujours originaux!*"

"Do you wear a surgical jacket to dinner parties, Dr. Gautier?" Terry smiled. "I don't have definite hours here — but, believe me,

I wear a nurse's uniform during the day."

"Then I am to believe that you are now at liberty?"

"More or less." Oddly, Terry had given no previous thought to the fact that there was no line drawn here between working hours and her free time. She hovered somewhere between an always available lackey and a totally independent member of the Olner family, and she said as much to the doctor.

Armand Gautier's face clouded. "But this is absurd! You must assert yourself. Otherwise, especially if you have no . . ." He waved his hands impatiently, searching for the right word. "If you have not a man to escort you, and you cannot call one hour your own, how can you enjoy my wonderful country?"

Terry shrugged. "That's probably a good question, Doctor."

"But, happily, you have meet Armand Gautier! *Voyons!* I will place myself at your service, *oui?*"

"I . . . don't know. You . . ." Torn between bewilderment and laughter at the man's expression, Terry settled for drawing a deep breath. Dr. Gautier looked as though he had just saved the world from extinction in the nick of time. "I imagine you're a . . . very busy man. You can't spare . . ."

65

"For what is important, a man will find the time. I speak . . . how shall I say? *En mauvais anglais,* I fear. Nevertheless, I address myself to the heart of the matter, with no hypocrisies. It would give me great pleasure to assume this agreeable duty." Dr. Gautier whipped a leather-bound appointment book from inside his jacket, thumbed through its scribbled pages swiftly, and then placed a forefinger on a blank spot. "I am available tomorrow evening. *Et de plus . . .*" There was more knit-browed concentration and thumping of pages. ". . . *de plus,* tomorrow afternoon . . . and the following afternoon . . . and one afternoon more later." He snapped the book shut, replaced it with a flourishing wave of his arm, and asked earnestly, "Will this be convenient, mademoiselle, or would you wish to make another suggestion?"

Terry felt her eyes opening wide. "I don't think I know . . . exactly when you . . ."

"If you do not know," Dr. Gautier said authoritatively, "then the responsibility is falling upon me to decide, *non? Bien!* Tomorrow I will arrive precisely at the hour of seven and you will decide here the matter of your dinner. This is already arrange." He clapped his hands together in a motion that indicated he had solved another earth-shattering problem, turning, in the next moment, toward the sound of Bill Lindley's footsteps on the stairway. "Ah, *mon ami le médecin.*"

Dr. Gautier assumed a rigid professional pose as Bill returned to the room. To look at his grave countenance, no one would have guessed that in the past few minutes he had taken control of a total stranger's social life. "The patient will see me, *docteur?* Or, he is perhaps . . ."

"Mr. Olner's awake," Bill said. He smiled vaguely at Terry. "Richard swears he wasn't asleep . . . just resting his eyes. With him it's an admission of weakness to acknowledge that he gets tired easily!"

Dr. Gautier nodded his approval. "A man of pride. I myself dislike to say that I do not have the inexhaustible vitality." He sighed as they started toward the stairway. "And, as you know, *docteur,* ours is not a profession for the weak man. Like you, I am, as you would say, the hard worker."

Fast worker, Terry corrected mentally. (A medical Charles Boyer. A good man in an emergency room. Even outside his surgical suite at the clinic, an "operator.")

CHAPTER 5

At a corner table near the bar, a small group of men, oblivious to the diners at the other five tables in the rustic inn, sang in soft harmony to the accompaniment of a guitar. There was a haunting, mellow quality in their voices and in their songs. Even to Terry's untrained ear, the lyrics did not sound French. She looked over her wine glass at Armand Gautier and asked if she were wrong.

"*Non,* you are correct, Terry. They are from the Basque country." Armand paused to concentrate on a few bars of the song. "Not French, but still *la belle chanson, oui?*" His finely molded face, which Terry had learned was an ever changing emotional barometer, brightened with an affectionate smile. "At times it is the case that we also import what is beautiful." Inside its amber glass, the single candle lighting their table flickered, its light softening Armand's already warm expression. "Will you permit me to tell you that your eyes are the color of spring violets?"

Terry thanked him for the compliment lightly, steering the conversation to safer subjects by asking a flood of questions. Was that old wine cask near the bar as ancient as it looked? How many years had it taken to cover this ceiling with empty, straw-wrapped bottles? Were the informally dressed people at the other tables Armand's friends? All of the other diners had nodded their recognition, but Armand had not stopped to introduce Terry — nor were the local patrons of the inn paying the faintest attention to the doctor and his date.

Armand disposed of the less personal questions quickly, throwing in for good measure the fact that the inn had been in continuous operation for nearly two hundred years, and that the open hutch opposite the stone fireplace (a ponderous dish cabinet Armand called a *"bahut Breton"*) dated back to a half century before that. But the young doctor's consummate interest was not in things, but in people.

"Everyone in this room is my friend and also, at one time or the other, my patient. Do they seem to you rude, to busy themselves with talk and not to notice me? Ah, but this is being French. To speak out when it is time to speak, and to be quietly discreet when it is plain that a man is in the company of a so lovely young lady."

Armand's eyes explored Terry's with a disturbing intimacy, and she thought, "We're back to *that* again."

To her relief, Armand elaborated on the subject of his fellow villagers. Most of the people were shopkeepers, teachers, or tradesmen; the fishermen from less affluent St. Juste came to Roberval only to shop or, under less fortunate circumstances, to visit the clinic.

"So I have many friends in the smaller village, also," Armand said. "And there, too, I would be granted the courtesy of . . . at a time like this . . . the privacy a man wishes for himself. A fine compliment, since I am not much more than a tourist myself. Here, if your great-great-grandfather was not born in the village, you are a . . . how do you say? . . . A newcomer."

"Is that what you are?" Terry asked.

"But of course! My family is in Paris. I am here by choice and not by birth." Armand looked fondly reflective for a moment. "Yet the people here have taken me to their hearts. Tonight they do not disturb me, but tomorrow! The village will psst-

70

psst-psst. . . ." Armand laughed his delight at the thought as he imitated gossiping mouths with his fingers. "Some will disapprove because their *médecin* is courting a girl who is not French; they are very provincial, these people. Others will see only how beautiful you are, as I do. When they know that you are also a nurse, they will be *enchantés!*"

It was a little disconcerting to think that she was being eyed as a prospective bride, when Terry had bargained for no more than a casual dinner date. And Armand had used the word "courting!" He had said it blandly, without embarrassment, as though the matter were taken for granted.

It was a relief, then, when Armand drove Terry back to the villa soon after their late dinner, explaining that he had to be up early the next morning for surgery. At the door, he kissed her forehead, but though he seemed unmistakably attracted to her, the kiss was a quick impulsive gesture that could not possibly be construed as anything but friendly. For Terry to have called off their beach date for the next afternoon would have been insulting, under the circumstances.

Besides, it had been a wonderful evening — the dinner delicious, the atmosphere

71

charming, the conversation interesting, especially when Armand was sidetracked from semiromantic talk and persuaded to discuss himself, his work, and his country. As Irene Washburn said when she was told about the date the next morning, "You got nothin' better goin' for you, honey. A good-lookin' doctor in the hand beats one in the bush any old day." (If she suspected Terry's unrequited love for Bill Lindley, Irene was at least as discreet as the villagers of Roberval, for she didn't mention the American doctor by name.)

Irene's reactions, however, were predictable, as were Carl's. ("It's about time you got outta the house. A doll like you oughta be out swingin' every night.") Reactions from the rest of the household were more unexpected and varied.

Tick could be discounted. He had raced off for Cannes in one of the leased Peugeots several hours before Armand came to call for Terry. Disappointingly, Bill Lindley had done the same thing earlier that morning; there wasn't even the faint hope of stirring a bit of jealous interest in him. Having placed his recuperating patient in the hands of a local doctor, he took off for a week of sightseeing, not even aware that Armand Gautier's interest in Terry was more than professional.

Wanda, lingering behind because of "important social commitments" (actually, a bridge game with the dull near-neighbors whom she considered "worth cultivating for their contacts"), showed surprising interest in Terry's date with the French doctor. She appeared incredulous when she saw Terry getting into Armand's little Renault. Her expressions the following morning were so kaleidescopic that Irene found them hilarious.

"Can you imagine the wheels going around in her nasty little head? She doesn't know whether to be relieved because you're not out to grab her daddy's money, or to hate you for being a double-crossing hussy. You know . . . stepping out on the guy you're plannin' to marry."

The very concept was ridiculous, of course, but it seemed an accurate explanation for Wanda's tight-lipped, resentful attitude later that morning and her contrasting, superfriendly question, "Did you have a good time last night?"

Terry said, "Yes, thank you," without providing any details.

Dissatisfied, Wanda continued her probe. "Dr. Gautier's awfully attractive."

It was obvious that Wanda was stepping

down from her previous snobbish position because she was consumed by curiosity. Perversely, Terry only smiled and said, "Yes, isn't he?"

Wanda's eyes narrowed. "He probably doesn't have a dime to his name. You can't get rich doctoring in a crummy village."

By that time, Terry was beginning to enjoy the game. "Oh, I don't know. The fees are small, but think of the volume. I understand Dr. Gautier delivered four babies just in the past week."

Realizing that she was being put down, Wanda ended her hopefully confidential talk and gave Terry a scathing look that, distilled, would have produced pure venom. She walked away without saying another word.

But hostility from Wanda was hardly a phenomenon. It was Richard Olner who puzzled Terry. When she had told him about her date the previous evening, he had appeared alternately crestfallen, indifferent, and edgy. This morning, he was inordinately cheerful and almost pathetic in his attempt to demonstrate his progress toward recovery.

Walking out to the walled garden at the rear of the villa, Richard declined the support of Terry's arm. "If you want to . . . sit down and hold hands, I'm . . . willing. But

I'm maneuvering . . . just fine now, wouldn't you say?"

"You're doing beautifully," Terry assured him.

"I'll be getting . . . rid of the cane soon," Richard said. His speech was still hesitant, but he no longer had to search for words with which to express himself. With the sunlight glinting from his blond hair and with his exuberant manner, he seemed younger than his forty-six years.

When they had settled in lawn chairs near a cluster of thick palm trees, Richard said, "I'm following Bill's orders, to . . . take it easy while he's gone. Next week, though . . . we want to . . . start getting around. No more of . . . what I did last night — killing time playing . . . gin rummy with the Washburns."

Terry felt a slight pang of guilt. "Is that what you did?"

"Everybody else . . . ran out on me." Richard's look was mildly accusing. "Understand, I . . . don't blame you. Gautier's a . . . personable chap and he . . . certainly knows the area. As long as I'm not up to . . . showing you around, I'd have to be a . . . slave-driver to resent your . . . doing a little sightseeing." It was clear that he looked upon Armand Gautier as no more than a casual tourist guide. "You've been . . . a treasure about sacrificing your own good times to . . . look after me. I'm going to . . . as I've said . . . make it up to you, Terry. Believe me! We'll fly to Paris and . . . see Paris like it's never been seen before. Next week, we'll . . . start with Monaco . . . and . . . really tear up the Riviera."

He was far from being ready to "tear up" any place in the world, but it would have been cruel to tell him so.

"Whatever your doctor says," Terry said.

Richard laughed shortly. "You mean my . . . doctors. Plural. They're . . . ganging up on me, Terry, but . . . I've got news for them. They're both going to be . . . superfluous in a . . . week or so."

"I'm sure Bill wouldn't have gone away for a whole week if he thought you needed him," Terry said. "And Armand certainly thinks you're in good shape." She paused, not quite certain of how to tell Richard that she wanted part of the afternoon off. "He's . . . offered to do a little more tour-guiding for a few hours this afternoon. Will you mind?"

Richard's face fell. "You're going . . . out with him again?" He qualified his disapproval hastily. "It's fine . . . fine with me. Makes me feel less guilty about . . . all the

76

overtime you've put in. I . . . feel like I've . . . exploited you."

"Nonsense. I can't possibly say that I've been earning my salary lately."

Richard beamed at the suggestion that he was well enough to make life easy for his nurse. "Well, don't get . . . qualms of conscience about it, Terry. I . . . don't want you getting bored here and . . . walking out before I . . . before I'm . . ."

There was a suspenseful moment before Terry realized that the confusion was completely normal. Richard was not having difficulty in transposing thoughts into words; apparently he had something on his mind, but was not quite sure of what he wanted to say at the moment. There was a vast difference, and Terry relaxed as the sentence was completed.

"Well, look, it's a little . . . premature to talk about my plans now. You go ahead and . . . enjoy yourself. While I'm waiting for . . . Bill to get back, I'll have plenty to occupy me."

Was he asking her to feel sorry for him because he felt neglected? Seeking sympathy wasn't typical of Richard. "Going out with Dr. Gautier isn't really important to me. If you're going to be bored here this afternoon, I . . ."

"No, no, no . . . you go right ahead," Richard insisted. He seemed pleased to hear that the date had no personal meaning to Terry. "You may as well enjoy yourself. I . . . want to spend some time talking to . . . Wanda, for one thing. And squaring a few matters with my attorney. No, I won't have . . . time on my hands. Plenty to do."

Terry was dubious. "Playing gin with Carl and Irene?"

Richard laughed. "I wish it were . . . going to be that simple, dear." He changed the subject abruptly, then, telling Terry he had decided to ease the dual staff problem by taking the Washburns along as personal help on a projected series of trips. "I'm thinking of this villa as a . . . point of departure," Richard explained. "We're going to have a . . . wonderful time, Terry. One more week . . ."

Richard clung to that arbitrary time span, as though everything that had been wrong would suddenly be righted at the end of seven more days, and Terry said nothing to discourage him. It was his determination to look ahead that had produced such miraculous results; if he was convinced that he would be ready to increase his activity in one more week, he would probably be right.

For a short period after their conversation

in the garden, Terry felt vaguely uneasy about Richard's plans and the fact that all of them seemed to be centered around her. Most unsettling had been the meaningful light in his eyes when he talked about "squaring a few matters" with his attorney and talking to Wanda. Was it Terry's imagination, or had there been a direct message in the way Richard had looked at her?

Yet it was all too insubstantial for concern. Terry forgot the matter completely moments after Armand Gautier drove up the curving driveway, tooting the horn of his Renault in unprofessional enthusiasm when he saw her waiting for him on the terrace. She was only aware that Richard Olner and his daughter had been closeted in the *petit* salon when she stepped out of the villa — only faintly concerned with the fact that she had heard her name mentioned twice in the few seconds it had taken to pass by the salon door.

CHAPTER 6

"How good that you are not the rich tourist," Armand said lazily. He slid lower down in the canvas bench that took up most of what passed for passenger space in the tiny fishing sloop. He lifted his arm to protect Terry from a sudden spray of water tossed back from the prow. "If you were one of those what you call 'jets sets,' I would have a great problem to entertain you."

"You're doing beautifully," Terry assured him. Her pullover and shorts were almost soaked through, and her hair undoubtedly looked like a black mop dipped in salt water and rearranged by a stiff breeze, but neither the "captain," his teen-aged crew of one, nor Armand seemed to be concerned, and neither was she.

She felt an exhilaration; after the dreariness of catering to a nervous, strong-willed patient, after being humiliated by his son and daughter, and after nights of futile dreaming about a man who barely knew she existed, it gave her a glorious feeling of freedom to be sailing aimlessly along the coast.

Terry turned her face up to the warm sun and the refreshing spray, grinning as Armand launched another of his seriocomic analyses of his "responsibility" to her.

"I ask myself, what would a beautiful young girl, not rich, but with much appreciation . . . what would she enjoy to do?" Armand went on. "One must consider these matters, *n'est-ce pas?*"

"She'd like looking at *that*," Terry told him. Her eyes followed the shoreline on their left, a flawless picture of blue water exploding into silver plumes against the palisades — pastel, tile-roofed villas and humbler whitewashed cottages starkly outlined against rich green-black masses of vegetation. Around them, the sea glinted its jewel colors — turquoise, sapphire, aquamarine — and their voices competed only with the sound of gently slapping waves and the occasional shrill cry of a gull. "She'd enjoy doing exactly this," Terry murmured.

Armand nodded gravely. He had applied the same solemn concern during all of their dates over the past week. His free hours were precisely timed. And because they were so limited, he was determined to make every second a momentous one.

Lolling on the beach at St. Juste, he had been convinced that Terry would be happier doing something more active. Teaching her to water-ski, he had worried that she was not seeing enough of the typical village life. In a half dozen outdoor cafés and picturesque bistros, and, again, during a tour of the clinic at Roberval, he had decided that Terry could not possibly go on without seeing the color of St. Tropez.

While they were dancing to rock and roll in a dim hangout for the bizarrely costumed American hippie crowd that had taken over that once-fashionable resort town, Armand made an abrupt decision: tomorrow morning he would engage the little sloop of one of his former patients. He was certain that Terry was disappointed because she had not seen the Cote d' Azur from a typical fishing vessel. Now, skirting the Riviera, he was assessing the sights Terry had not seen.

"Some of the fault is with Monsieur Olnair," Armand said. "At this time, which he choose to come, the Carnival in Nice is finished. The racing season at the Hippodrome at Cagnes-sur-Mer is also completed and will not resume until the night races in July. In any case, I cannot afford the time or yet the money to visit the places you have surely looked forward to visit . . . the restaurant Eden Roc at Cap d'Antibes, the casinos . . ."

"I didn't come here looking forward to . . . plush places," Terry argued. "Armand, why can't you relax and let me enjoy what we're doing right now?"

"You are not miserable?"

Terry laughed at the doleful, doubtful tone. "*Miserable?* This is like a crazy dream for me."

Their skipper had taken a new tack, and there was no longer any need for Armand to pretend that he was protecting Terry from the salt spray. He leaned closer, his dark eyes sultry and, at the same time, burning with an intense light. "Then you are happy to be with me?"

Terry's breath quickened. Whatever reply she gave might be misinterpreted. Already hunched low, Terry edged downward, uncomfortably close to the wet planking. With Armand's face almost touching hers, she could think of nothing to say that would neither insult nor encourage him.

Armand mistook her silence for acceptance. His lips brushed her damp forehead for only a moment. In the next micro-instant, he had pressed his lips against Terry's 'in a strangely gentle kiss. "I have misjudge you, *chère amie,*" he said softly. "You are not like the others I see, who come to satiate themselves with less simple pleasures. We are very close, you and I. You have become most dear to me."

A sudden gust of wind jerked the small boat forward, throwing Armand to the floor. The sloop's owner, who had been discreetly ignoring his unaccustomed passengers until then, laughed. The young crewman scrambled to help Armand back to his perch on the crude bench. In the general laughter and discussion that followed, the brief, intimate spell was shattered. Terry forestalled another by getting to her feet and pretending a consuming interest in sailing.

Armand translated Terry's questions and the fisherman's replies. His Gallic instinct for romantic matters undoubtedly told him that the magic moment was gone.

He was too fine a person, Terry decided — too openhearted and sincere — to be toyed with. Armand's interest in her was plainly as serious as it had been sudden; after that kiss, any continued show of warmth on her part would be construed as encouragement.

Several times, as Armand drove her from the St. Juste quay to the villa, Terry made a stab at telling the young doctor how she felt about him. Between her own inadequate supply of words that would make the explanation as painless as possible, and Armand's enthusiastic interruptions, Terry accomplished nothing.

Without referring to the abrupt gust of wind that had disrupted a tender moment between them, Armand dutifully filled Terry in on the gregales, unbelievably sudden windstorms of near-hurricane proportions that occasionally plagued Mediterranean sailors at this time of the year. As he pulled the Renault to a stop on the villa's circular driveway, he flashed a mischievous smile. "Now you will be fearful to go sailing with me again. And I will not know if you are afraid of the gregale, or of Armand Gautier."

Terry forced a smile in return. She was too self-conscious — too conscious of Wanda Olner, who was sunning herself on the terrace nearby — to give Armand a straight answer.

Once again, Armand interpreted the lack of a reply as a reply in itself. "I have not frighten you, then? *Bien!* I am not free tomorrow. Tomorrow, in my little book, is one duty after the other, the morning until the night. This is in order that we can once again be together. This time, with no one to laugh if I . . . how you say . . . 'fall for you,' *oui?*"

He was chuckling at his own wit as he helped Terry out of the car. "Can we say I will come for you in the evening? At seven o'clock? Not to sail. I have already an idea more *magnifique* for us than to . . ."

"I can't," Terry said quietly. She avoided Armand's eyes, knowing that he would be hurt no matter what excuse she gave. "I've . . . been spending too much time away from my patient as it is."

"Monsieur Olnair has the objection if you take a few hours for your own pleasure?" Armand's voice rose to a disturbing pitch.

Terry kept hers to a near whisper. "It's not that, Armand. I just . . . it's not fair to . . . to let you think I . . ."

"You would prefer to be with your patient than with me? Even when it is not a matter of duty?" Armand's tone hovered now between misery and indignation. He drew himself up to his full height. "It is not my habit to impose myself, mademoiselle!"

There were more words; Terry remembered them only vaguely afterward. Whatever she said failed to soften the blow, and when Armand took his leave, the slammed car door and the screech of rubber tires as he turned down the hill testified to his mood.

Sick inside, Terry hoped to cross the terrace and escape to her room without having to exchange more words with Wanda Olner. It was a futile hope. As Terry moved toward the door, Wanda tossed her cigarette into a clump of ivy and sat up in her lounge chair. "I guess I shouldn't ask if you had fun," she said.

Terry glanced in her direction long enough to note that Wanda's eyeshadow matched the poison-green piping on her paisley sundress. Acutely aware of her disheveled appearance, Terry looked longingly at the door. "I had a wonderful time," she said.

"But you're not about to go out with him again, is that it?" Wanda got to her feet, stretching her arms before her in an appropriately feline gesture and yawning. "Sorry — I couldn't help hearing your boyfriend's sad lament. Or . . . wondering why you'd give up a date with someone that attractive to . . . maybe play cards with a wracked-up old man?"

Terry had started to walk away from the presumptuous questioning. She stopped in her tracks and turned at the ugly reference to Richard Olner. "I don't think of your father as a 'wracked-up old man.' He's a patient who's making a very courageous recovery."

Wanda was staring at her with unconcealed venom. "Meaning it's time you started paying attention to him again? You can always take up where you left off with Dr. Gautier when you've cinched your deal with my dad. Right?"

"I don't know what you're talking about." Terry made a determined move away from the girl — then gasped as Wanda grabbed her arm, spinning her around.

"You listen to me! Tick and I saw through you the minute we laid eyes on you! You've got my dad so wrapped up in you, you figure you can even run around with other men and count on him to marry you. Well, don't be too sure of yourself. When I tell him . . ."

"What are you going to tell him?" Terry asked evenly. She was grateful that, for once, she was able to control the tears with which she usually expressed her rage. "I have exactly one obligation to your father, Miss Olner. I fulfilled that obligation for months at the hospital in New York, when . . . just incidentally, you and your brother were too busy elsewhere to come and visit him. I've had less to do here, I'll admit that. But your father and his doctor think my services are still needed, and that's why I'm here. What I do in my free time doesn't concern them, and it concerns you even less!"

Wanda's face remained a study in contemptuous disbelief. "You sell your phony story very cleverly. Too bad I'm not buying."

Terry brushed past the girl, too disgusted to carry on the ridiculous argument. If Wanda was convinced that her father was being victimized, only time would cure her sick imagination. "Believe anything you like," Terry muttered. "I couldn't care less." She felt Wanda's almost palpable, hate-filled gaze on her back all the way to the door.

Shortly before dinner, Terry looked down from her bedroom window to see one of the Peugeots racing up the road. She was breathless for a few moments, then released her disappointment in a weary sigh as Tick Olner stepped out of the car, snapping his fingers and shouting something inaudible to Carl Washburn. If Carl was in the garage, and if he heard the rude summons, he made a point of ignoring it; Tick came up the stairs a few minutes later, cursing the "insolent trash" his father put up with.

Tick's return from a tour of the gambling casinos had one positive feature: Terry's suggestion that Richard might like to have a private "family reunion" dinner with his son and daughter was accepted gratefully.

"That's typically thoughtful of you," Richard said. "They'll both be running out as . . . soon as dinner's over, I'm . . . sure, and I do have a few matters to discuss with the kids."

Apart from her distaste for sitting at the dinner table with the younger Olners, Terry yearned for a period of being alone. The incident with Armand Gautier had depressed her; she had handled the situation badly, returning his hospitality and affection with a curtness that was just short of slapping the young doctor's face. (*Would she feel less guilty if she wrote him a friendly, explanatory note?*)

Then, too, the situation with Wanda was becoming intolerable. Wasn't it stupid, even masochistic, to expose herself to more shoddy arguments like the one on the terrace? For what purpose — an occasional glimpse of Bill Lindley, who would probably drop in to see Richard a few times before going back to New York?

Write the apologetic letter to Armand, summon the courage to tell Richard you're quitting, phone for a plane reservation and . . .

Richard was saying something to her.

Terry shook herself out of her gloomy introspection, hearing the end of his sentence: ". . . looking forward to a quiet evening with you, Terry. As soon as the kids leave, can we get together?"

Ironically, Terry remembered seeing the same wistful, half pleading expression etched across Armand Gautier's more sensitive face just a few hours ago.

"It's terribly important to me," Richard emphasized.

Terry noticed that he was making a concerted effort to stand up tall, without the use of his cane.

"Terribly important to both our futures," he said.

He was looking directly at Terry, more steady on his feet than she was as she promised to join him in the *petit* salon as soon as they had the villa to themselves.

CHAPTER 7

A full hour before Terry was to hear the message that was important to Richard Olner's future and to her own, she was given a preview by Irene Washburn.

While the Olners were at the dinner table, Irene came to Terry's room, confiding in a not-too-subdued tone that "Mr. O. just launched World War Three downstairs. Listen . . . they're screamin' at each other like banshees."

Terry set aside the notepaper on her desk. She had got as far as, "Dear Armand," then drawn a blank. "What's it about?" she asked carelessly.

"I dunno, but I think Mr. O. just told his brats he's gonna get married again, whether they like it or not." Irene's round face assumed an injured expression. "How come you didn't let me and Carl know, honey? Ain't we your friends no more?"

Terry gaped at her, incredulous. "Maybe I

haven't told you because . . . this is the first I've heard of it."

Irene punched Terry's arm in a playful gesture. "Aw, come on, kid! The boss wouldn't be tellin' Wanda to get off your back if he wasn't pretty doggone sure of himself. When I come up the steps, he was tellin' her he wanted you treated with respect. Not just 'cause you're a nurse, but because you're gonna be part of the family. Try an' tell me this is news to you."

"I'll swear it, Irene!" Terry shook her head, like a sleeper trying to break out of an impossible dream. "He said he wanted to talk to me tonight . . . about something important. And he . . . well, he looked like he may have had something like that on his mind. But . . . to assume that I'm going to accept! Isn't that about as presumptuous as a man can get?"

Irene had a more sympathetic view. "Maybe he's just clearin' the path, in case you grab the bait. Y'know, you could do a lot worse, Terry. You could waste your whole life dreamin' about some guy you can't have, an' pass up . . . well, take me, f'rinstance. I had a choice between marryin' Carl Washburn an' droolin' over Cary Grant's picture on my dresser. Maybe Carl ain't much, but Cary wasn't sendin' me no

93

roses every Valentine's Day, if you know what I mean."

Terry knew exactly what she meant. But knowing the futility of her love for Bill Lindley — that had nothing to do with her answer to the predicted proposal later that evening.

She listened quietly and patiently, her insides churning with a mixture of pity and resentment as Richard Olner presented his case, giving her a point-by-point monologue in favor of their marriage — exactly, Terry assumed, as he might have offered arguments favoring a merger of his company with another to a board of directors.

Seated beside Terry on one of the velvet-covered sofas, Richard climaxed his speech by reaching for her hand. "Please don't think you're going to . . . have to compete with anyone in . . . this arrangement, dear. My first two wives claimed I . . . neglected them because I was . . . married to my business. Maybe they were right, although . . . neither of them ever voiced a . . . complaint about the comforts that business brought them."

Terry closed her eyes for a moment, wondering, *What does this have to do with me?*

"Well, I just wanted to . . . assure you that

94

you won't ever have that problem," Richard went on. His speech was still punctuated by pauses, but Terry couldn't help feeling a strong admiration for the man, remembering that only a few months ago he had been barely able to express himself at all. "They say a . . . man doesn't learn to appreciate life until he . . . comes close to losing it. You've seen for yourself that . . . that applies to me. I'm going to . . . start living, Terry. Really living. Enjoying the . . . fruits of all that . . . killing effort. I want you to . . . share all the benefits, without having to . . . carry any of the old burdens. Travel, see the world. Not miss a . . . good bet anywhere, that's what I . . . want us to do. Now, then . . ."

It's almost as though he's reading a statement prepared by his lawyer, Terry thought. Her hand felt warm and uncomfortably damp pressed between Richard's palms, yet she couldn't withdraw it now without creating an awkward scene. *Let him finish. In his own way, he's completely sincere. It's only fair to hear him out and then . . . let him down as gracefully as possible.*

"I was coming to the . . . matter of my . . . son and daughter," Richard continued. "I realize that they . . . haven't been as pleasant to you as they . . . might be, Terry. You've

95

been exceptionally understanding, probably because . . . well, you've . . . been around people. You know how . . . petty jealousies arise, especially within a family . . . a broken family. I won't . . . go into all that. What I . . . do want you to know, is that I've been . . . completely frank and . . . completely firm with the kids. They know . . . what my intentions are. They've been told precisely what arrangements I've asked my attorney to make regarding their . . . financial future and yours . . ."

"Richard, I . . ."

"Please hear me out, Terry. This is an important aspect that will save a great deal of bickering and . . . uncertainty for all of you. I know you find it embarrassing to discuss finances, but we've got to be realistic. I'm looking forward to a long, happy life with you, darling, and we'll get to the more . . . pleasant aspects in a moment."

As if he had been reminded of the "pleasant aspects," Richard let go of Terry's hand and managed to slide an arm across the back of the sofa, the sleeve of his jacket barely touching Terry's neck. "Let's get these necessary details out of the way first," he persisted. "As I say, I'm not taking a . . . pessimistic view. Not at all. I'm feeling . . . better now than . . . I ever did before. But we're . . . all of us only . . . mortals. I've . . . had one stroke. Just . . . in case, Terry. I want you to know . . . the day we're married, you'll be . . . financially set for life, no matter what . . . happens to me. And with no . . . possible interference from . . . any of my other heirs."

It was impossible to go on listening to him. Shaking inside, Terry felt nothing but pity now for this strangely driven man who had glossed over the only words that a marriage proposal required, saying, "I love you, Terry" with only a degree more of passion than he was now injecting into his financial disclosures. "Richard . . ." She made a concerted effort to keep her voice calm and unemotional. "I know you didn't want to be interrupted until . . ."

"Until I've convinced you that we'd be . . . very happy together," he said.

Terry shook her head. "You don't understand. You don't have to 'convince' someone who loves you. I'm sorry. I wish you hadn't made this necessary."

For a moment Terry was fearful that her patient was on the verge of another stroke. "You're telling me you . . . wouldn't even consider me as . . . as a . . ."

"I know I have a great deal of admiration for you," Terry said. "You're one of the bravest, most tenacious, most . . . pleasant people I've ever seen through a major illness. But it's not fair to let you go on selling an idea that . . . I can't possibly buy."

If she had expected Richard to give up his cause and sink into despondency, Terry was wrong. "Why not?" he demanded. "You have to . . . give me logical reasons. Is it my age? Forty-six isn't old. A few more weeks at the rate I've been . . . picking up energy, I'll run circles around my own son. My illness? You know it's . . . a temporary thing. I'm a fighter, Terry. Every day I . . ."

"I know," Terry said gently. She didn't have to be reminded that a lesser man might have resigned himself to the state of a human vegetable; the very strength of Richard's argument was proof of his recovery. "I'm not thinking of you as a helpless old man, please believe me. It's not that at all."

"Then what . . . unless there's someone else I haven't . . . heard about, what reason could you possibly . . ."

"I'm not in love with you," Terry said. "It's that simple, and there's nothing either of us can do to change it."

"But that's not . . . not true!" Richard cried. He was gazing at Terry as though she had said something utterly ridiculous. "Love! Love's a . . . relative matter. Everyone has a . . . different definition for love. I've learned how . . . empty that starry-eyed, romantic nonsense is . . . when you have to start living with someone. I say, when two people have . . . mutual trust and . . . respect for each other . . ."

". . . they have the basis for a good friendship," Terry concluded. "But that's all, Richard. In my case, I respect you enough not to be evasive. I've told you exactly how I feel, and . . . I wouldn't have been that honest if I'd thought it necessary to patronize you."

"I see." Richard's face looked old and haggard, suddenly. "I appreciate your . . . withholding pity, Terry. I don't want anyone to . . . feel sorry for me. Ever."

An eternity later, it was over. But not before Terry had agreed to stay on as his nurse for at least another month. He had insisted that her presence was necessary to his recovery — to his morale. He had hinted that, now that he was better able to get around, she would see him in a less depressing context; he would make her want to be at his side. She would learn to love him.

These were the very arguments that should have made her want to escape. And, ironically, Terry made the promise to stay because she did indeed feel sorry for him.

Because, in his own peculiar way, Richard Olner probably loved her as much as he was capable of loving anyone — and needed her more than he was willing to admit.

One month . . . two. Any friend could make that small sacrifice. Especially when (*be honest, be honest!*) . . . especially when the man's doctor was due back at the villa any hour now.

CHAPTER 8

Bill Lindley did not return the next day, nor the day after. As Irene put it, in her inimitably blunt fashion, he was "prob'ly havin' himself a ball with them rich babes over in Nice." She pronounced the name of that Riviera showplace to rhyme with "dice," but Terry was not amused. There was too much truth in what Irene had said to prompt any joyous reaction.

Without Armand Gautier to distract her mind, and with Richard working furiously to prove that he was, in truth, a strong, virile, cheerful, and youthful marriage prospect, the villa became a vast mausoleum in which Terry felt herself trapped. Why, when it was obvious that Richard didn't intend to take no for an answer — why hadn't she made the break immediately after that disturbing proposal? Staying on as his nurse only encouraged Richard's conviction that a little more time, a bit more positive pressure, was needed, and Terry would "see the light" as he saw it.

If Terry needed any proof that her employer had not given up the idea of marrying her, it was furnished by Wanda. If Richard's daughter had been told that his proposal had been rejected, Terry might have expected, if not a warmer attitude from Wanda, at least one that was less belligerent. Wanda hadn't been told anything of the kind. She had been cautioned to show "respect" for her father's future wife; she had been told how the Olner fortune would be divided to include Terry — and there, unquestionably, the matter stood. Wanda reacted by ignoring Terry completely, passing her in the villa's corridors without saying a word, and, finally, two days after her suspicions should have been permanently squashed, taking off for Monaco with her new friends from Texas. She, at least, was not around to aggravate Terry's misery.

Tick Olner more than made up for his sister's absence. At first, Terry assumed that his overtly chummy attitude was grounded in fact; wasn't it logical that Tick could afford to be more human now that his inheritance was no longer threatened? Certainly Richard had told his son that Terry had no interest in becoming the third Mrs. Olner!

This was a logical first impression, but during the next few days, as Tick's attentions became less and less brotherly, Terry found herself with a new unwelcome "admirer" on her hands.

"You sure got yourself a new add-on to your fan club," Carl observed one morning, while Terry was having breakfast in the kitchen with the Washburns. "If that punk kid starts gettin' too fresh, say the word, kiddo. I may be short, but puny I ain't."

Carl was bragging about his ancestry ("I come from a long line of champeen carnival wrestlers") when Irene cut in. "I got a better idea. If you can't get Junior to leave you alone, drop the word to Mr. O. That'll do it."

It might be the other way around, Terry decided. As Tick started becoming as pestiferous as his namesake, following her around the villa, suggesting going to the beach together in the evening, pouring unwanted drinks, managing to brush close to her at every possible opportunity, and making faintly suggestive remarks, it occurred to Terry that Tick's "friendliness" was contrived — perhaps even plotted by Wanda.

Irene agreed. "Ain't that a pip? Even if Mr. O. told them two jackals you don't want no part of joinin' the family, they wouldn't believe it. They couldn't see anybody passin' up a easy buck. So maybe they figure you're just playin' hard to get."

Carl wrinkled his puckish face in confusion. "You two babes are too deep for me. I don't get it."

"Stupid! Look, they tried everything else. Now, suppose they could show the boss that Terry's a floozy? That she wouldn't turn down a younger guy if he made a pass at her? They wouldn't have to worry no more about . . ."

"This is getting silly," Terry protested. "It's my own fault, actually. I ought to start packing tonight and stop this asinine wondering about who's planning to do what to whom. I hate to hurt Mr. Olner, but isn't it crazy to be the central figure in a big fat intrigue when I don't really care for any of these people?"

Carl and Irene made no comment. If they knew the answer to that question, they minded their own business, turning the conversation to a discussion of the one-week-on-one-week-off arrangement that had resolved Irene's feud with the French cook. They were looking forward to a go at the Riviera's gambling casinos next week, and as Carl observed, "You don't needa parlay-voo in French to shoot craps good."

He added a sincere willingness to "skip the whole deal, though, if you don't think you can handle the wolf alone."

Totally absurd. Pack and get out. What are you waiting for? For Bill to come back and remind you that you didn't mean anything to him?

Terry pondered the question throughout the day, avoiding anything that resembled a personal conversation with Richard Olner and retiring to her room early that evening when she heard Dr. Gautier was expected.

Avoiding Armand was as senseless as everything else she was doing. She hadn't found the words with which to explain her actions to the young doctor, and now an encounter with him would be doubly embarrassing. Terry began the tearful, half-hearted process of packing her clothes for the trip home.

It was nearly ten o'clock when she heard Armand leaving. He had stayed more than two hours, probably playing chess with Richard; both had an affinity for the game. Then, finding herself sleepless another hour later, Terry threw a robe over her pajamas and descended the staircase in the hope of finding the Washburns still awake. Even inane conversation with Carl and Irene was better than feeling unbearably restless and alone.

Richard had apparently gone to sleep, and Tick Olner had gone out earlier in the evening; if he was true to form, he wouldn't be home before dawn. Disappointingly, there was no stirring downstairs, either; the carefree carnies had gone to their room in the servants' quarters adjoining the garage.

Terry stood for a moment looking out across the terrace through the French windows in the larger salon. A luminous three-quarter moon bathed the garden in an eerie, golden light. Its path could be traced on the sea, Terry thought, it would be a sight to take home in memory. She pushed the glass-paneled door open and stepped outside.

It was incredibly beautiful here, with the moonlight filtered through the olive branches. A heavy funereal scent, probably that of the waxy white tuberoses edging the driveway, added to her melancholy mood. Nights like this were agonizing when you were in love and alone. Still, the emptiness of her room was less appealing. Terry started toward the low wall from which the moon's path on the Mediterranean would be visible.

"This beats Brooklyn, doesn't it?"

Terry froze at the startling closeness of the sound, recognizing Tick Olner's lazy intonation immediately.

She turned to see that she had passed within a few feet of Tick without noticing him. He was sprawled in one of the lounge chairs, his face half hidden by the shadow of palm fronds.

As Terry debated about hurrying back to the door, Tick pulled himself out of the lounge, carefully hanging onto the highball glass in his hand. He got up and moved slowly into the light; Terry saw that he was wearing formal dinner attire. His white tie had been yanked loose for comfort. Under the yellowish light, his face looked, strangely, like an older, dissipated replica of Richard's.

"I saw your light was on," Tick said. He spoke in a low, strained, oily tone, probably not anxious to waken his father. "I wondered when you'd be coming out here."

"I . . . wanted to talk to the Washburns," Terry told him.

"Sure you did." Tick moved closer, his hazel eyes reflecting an amused disbelief. "They're always out here going on midnight."

"No, I . . ." Terry felt herself blushing in confusion, and suddenly the very thought angered her. "Look, I don't have to explain every move I make to you. It's a beautiful night. I wanted . . ."

"A little company?" Tick swayed slightly on his feet. His voice had an insinuating quality now, and Terry wished she had obeyed her first impulse to escape even a brief contact with him. "Heard me come home, uh? Get a little lonesome up there all by yourself?" Tick was close enough now so that his alcoholic breath superseded the heavy scents permeating the air. He tottered as he leaned down to set his glass on a marble garden bench. As he straightened up, he purred, "I don't blame you, baby. Cooped up all day with my old man . . . I don't blame you at all."

"I'm not interested in your opinions," Terry said curtly. "If I had known you were here . . ."

"Oh, come off it, beautiful. I'm a big boy. I know what big girls are like."

Terry turned her back on him, starting for the door. "You disgust me," she said.

They had been standing in the exact spot where Terry had turned away, several days earlier, from an equally aggravating encounter with Wanda. This time, too, her departure was stopped by a restraining hand upon her arm.

"Don't play it coy with me, sugar. You knew I was down here. I left that crummy party early for this."

Tick's words were accompanied by a swift motion, pulling Terry into his arms. As he pressed his face closer to hers, she struggled, her revulsion expressing itself in white-hot fury. "Let go of me, you insolent . . . creep, you! Did you hear what I said? Let me go, or I'll let out a scream that'll . . ."

The snakelike grip tightened around her. "Relax! Relax, hon. You haven't had much fun lately. You can level with me, Terry. We've been wasting a lot of valuable time!"

Terry made one final effort to free herself, a futile effort, as Tick Olner's mouth smashed down upon hers in a sickeningly moist kiss. Pinned helplessly against him, she felt as though she would explode with rage, and when Tick lifted his lips from hers, still holding her fast in his arms, his short, patronizing laugh triggered the fuse. "Let me *go!*" she cried. "I don't want to . . . upset your dad, but if you don't take your hands off me, I'll . . ."

"You heard her, punk. Let her go!"

Tick's arms stiffened — then fell to his side as he whirled in the direction of Carl's voice.

Breathless, near tears, Terry looked past

Tick Olner to see Carl approaching from the little apartment next to the garage. He was still some distance away, a welcome but somewhat ludicrous figure with his old-fashioned white nightshirt outlined by a light from inside the open door behind him.

Carl's toga-like costume, his tousled hair and sleep-heavy, round blue eyes, must have looked hilarious to Tick. "Oh, wow! Nero to the rescue!"

There was nothing funny about Carl's stance as he drew nearer. His small fists were clenched and held upward, ready for an attack. Even in the dim light, his face was dark with anger. "You been askin' for a rap in the mouth, Junior. It's gonna be my pleasure."

Tick made one of his familiar snorting sounds. "Cool it, hero. I might get shook if that big walrus you're married to came at me, but you don't scare . . ."

Carl dived forward; his fist swung upward in a wide arc. At least two inches shorter than Tick, he missed his mark, fanning the air and spinning around in a stumbling half circle. He was charging again when Irene came puffing across the terrace, a formidable sight with her hair rolled up in monstrous pink plastic curlers and a faded blue flannel robe wrapped around her big body.

She stationed herself between her husband and his adversary like an immovable wall. "Don't go wastin' your energy on this jerk, Carl."

"Listen, you saw what he . . ."

"Forget it, Carl. There's other ways to put brats in their place."

A pair of headlights rose like twin suns over the curving hillside driveway. Terry caught her breath, but the others ignored the approaching car.

"Let's get outta here before we disturb Mr. O.," Irene said. "Maybe Junior don't have to get up in the morning, but the rest of us got work to do."

Either out of stubbornness or because Carl's abortive attack had startled him into immobility, Tick hadn't moved from the spot. Now his eyes gave Irene a sneering head-to-toe survey, and he muttered, "You won't be working around here long when I tell my dad about this." He ignored the slamming of a car door and the approaching footsteps. "He's put up with plenty from all three of you, but you aren't going to get away with trying to rough me up. She . . ." (He waved his thumb in Terry's direction.) ". . . invited me down here. She doesn't need a couple of clowns like you to keep her pure and holy. All I've ever had to do was snap my fingers and . . ."

Tick left his sentence dangling in mid air, seeing what Terry had already seen: Bill Lindley was standing on the edge of the terrace, a look of grave bewilderment on his face.

Carl turned around. "Oh, hi, Doc."

Irene echoed his words, and Terry nodded her head in acknowledgment. She wanted nothing more than to run from the shoddy scene.

"I don't know what's going on here," Bill said. His tone was hushed, but he was obviously annoyed. "Whatever it is, it's not going to help a man who's recovering from a cerebral accident. Can you battle it out somewhere where you aren't likely to waken . . ."

"Listen, I don't need a lecture from you, either!" Tick yelled. "All I was doing was having a little fun, and I didn't hear any objections from Terry, so . . ."

"That's not true!" Carl said softly.

". . . so I'm not taking any guff from the hired help around here," Tick went on.

He was threatening to have Terry and the Washburns fired, his voice rising to a shrill strident pitch, when Bill murmured, "I thought I told you to be quiet."

There was hardly a perceptible move on

112

Bill's part. One moment he was standing on the terrace with his arms at his side, and in the next there was a swift motion, a cracking sound like that of someone breaking a wooden lath, and Tick Olner was lying on the ground.

"Okay, get up and get out of here quietly," Bill said. "You can worry about getting me fired in the morning." His breath came hard, and a lock of hair had fallen over his forehead, but otherwise he was as calm as if he were greeting an apprehensive patient.

Tick's hand had gone to his mouth, and for a few seconds he remained sprawled on the tiled floor of the terrace. In a slow, hypnotic motion, he examined his hand, apparently expecting to find it covered with blood. It was not, and he brought it back to rub it across his jaw. His eyes avoided everyone present as he dragged himself to his feet. No one said a word until he had sulked to the front door, opened it, and disappeared inside the house.

Irene waddled across the terrace to close the door behind him.

"What we need," Carl said in a half whisper, ". . . what we need is a good stiff belt. Whatta ya say, Doc?"

Bill shook his head wearily. "That's all I'd need to put me out of commission for a week." He released a tired sigh. "I've just driven a long way, and I've been . . . pushing myself rather hard the past ten or twelve days."

"Livin' it up, hey?" Carl said approvingly. "Well, listen, we all need somethin' to calm us down. What say, Terry? We get Irene to fix us a couple nightcaps? Cocoa for the sissies."

"Count me with the sissies tonight," Bill said. For the first time he addressed Terry directly. "Join the party, Terry. I'd like to ask you how Richard's been progressing . . . how he's getting along with Dr. Gautier."

Approximately ten minutes later, Irene rose suddenly from the kitchen table, faking a tremendous yawn and insisting that she was too sleepy to stay up another second. Carl's announcement that he was "too stirred up to sleep" was corrected, after a judicious poke in the ribs from Irene. He trotted out of the room with her obediently, deciding that he was, after all, too tired to keep his eyes open.

There was a brief silence after their unsubtle departure, and Terry felt a moment of panic. This was one of those scenes she had constructed in her most wishful daydreams; she was alone with Bill in a charming setting. The dimly lighted, provincial kitchen had a romantic, other-worldly atmosphere. From where they sat, they could look over a quaintly arranged herb garden; the night was peaceful, the air balmy, the moonlight a touch of magic on the orange-tree branches framing the window. If Bill had nothing to say to her here, nothing but routine questions about Richard Olner's progress, he would never have anything to say to her. At least, nothing that she longed to hear.

He broke the quiet at long last, draining his cup of hot chocolate and saying, "I'd rather we didn't tell Richard what happened tonight. If you have any more trouble with Tick, let me know, Terry. I think I can manage him without upsetting his father."

Terry smiled at the understatement. "I noticed that, thank you."

Bill laughed a light, self-conscious laugh. "I didn't say that to make myself sound like a knight in shining armor. To be truthful, I've been looking for an excuse to give that kid a rap in the mouth since he was fifteen years old. I didn't see him often, but whenever Richard had him around I had itchy fists."

"I think that's a universal complaint," Terry said. "Anyway, I'm glad Carl was around. And that you came back when you did."

"It's not just a matter of keeping Richard calm," Bill said. "Though I can't overstress the importance of avoiding too much excitement. It's . . . well, knowing your importance to Richard and the idealized view he has of his offspring, I know he'd be terribly hurt by . . ." Bill shook his head and got up from the table abruptly. "It's late, and tomorrow's another day."

Terry had no choice but to agree, her heart sinking along with her last shred of hope. Bill escorted her to her door, said goodnight as he might have said it to anyone else in the world, and continued down the hall to his own room.

Two doors had closed between them before Terry permitted herself the luxury of tears.

CHAPTER 9

Carl and Irene Washburn had been replaced
for the week by their French counterparts,
and had gone off in search of "the nearest
crap game." Less than an hour ago, Bill had
driven off to some unannounced destina-
tion, and Wanda, barely returned from
Monaco, had dashed out again. Terry had
resigned herself to an evening of avoiding
Tick Olner and a few strained hours of
keeping her patient company.

There was little to do — nothing that
could absorb her or remove her aching
disappointment. It didn't help to know that
a few miles down the coast were fantasti-
cally beautiful resort cities that boasted
sweeping, tree-lined boulevards, glittering
restaurants, and every recreational facility
imaginable. There was even a country covering less than four hundred acres, complete
with a fairytale castle. Terry had visualized
herself whirling from one of these exciting

scenes to another, always with an adoring Bill Lindley at her side.

It had been a childish illusion, she realized now. And since she had made a reservation for her flight home the following Monday, there was nothing before her except the uncomfortable task of telling Richard that she could not keep her promise to him.

Terry had decided to make her announcement that evening, mentally rehearsing her approach all afternoon. She would have to be firm, avoiding any discussion of Richard's personal reasons for wanting her to stay. Toward evening, while Richard visited with his son, Terry watched a spectacular sunset from a stone viewing-point overlooking the sea, the words now solidly implanted in her mind: "You don't really need a special nurse any more, Richard. Dr. Gautier should certainly be able to recommend someone if . . ."

"Mademoiselle?"

Terry turned, feeling as though she had conjured up the French doctor by the mere process of mentioning his name. She had known he was expected to call on Richard after dinner. Now her embarrassment was magnified because it appeared obvious that she was avoiding Armand. She managed to stammer out a greeting, but her attempted apology was waved aside.

"I find it not to be believed," he said crisply.

"That I'm sorry? But I *am!*" Terry protested. "I didn't want to waste your time, but, then, I shouldn't have been so abrupt, running off without an explanation . . ."

"I am speaking of another matter," Armand interrupted. "When a woman does not wish to give a man hope, what is there to say? She does as she wishes, *n'est-ce pas? Non,* I have in mind to tell you that you cannot possibly do justice to St. Juste if you avoid the carnival there this evening. It is abominable that you should form your opinion of this so beautiful village and not observe the gala *fête* for which everyone here wait the full year."

"I wish I knew what you were talking about," Terry said.

"Better if you are shown," Armand told her. "You will hurry, *s'il vous plait,* to assume the blue dress in which I had my first sight of you. And a covering, also, for your shoulders, because we will no doubt be late. It will be not too warm in the fresh air by time for the fireworks."

Once again, Terry found it difficult not to smile at his imperious tone. Resplendent in a white summer suit that was undoubtedly his best, Armand was issuing his orders like a latter-day Napoleon. "Is that where everyone's gone?" Terry asked. "Miss Olner and . . . Dr. Lindley?"

"Who would not go? I have already told you, this is the event of greatest excitement." Armand made it clear that the invitation was an impersonal one. "I came, also, to ask if Monsieur Olnair did not wish for me to accompany him. For a short time only, of course. He is, however, engaged in a discussion from which he does not wish to excuse himself."

"Oh, he's just talking to . . ."

"I have reason to believe that he does not wish to be disturb," Armand said. His tone carried deep implications. "Also, I have taken the liberty to inform Monsieur Olnair that I will be happy to serve as your escort."

The man was unbelievable! "What did he say?"

"What can he say? Surely he does not wish for you to die of ennui?" Armand made an impatient motion with his hand. "Quickly. Already, I am certain, the band plays, and we will miss the parade."

No more than half an hour later, wearing the blue silk she had virtually been ordered to wear, Terry found herself clinging to the young doctor's arm as they pushed their

120

way through the crowded plaza of St. Juste. Rows of food-vending booths had sprung up like mushrooms around the small public square, and the air was redolent not only of flowers but of steaming bowls full of bouillabaisse, long crusty loaves of bread, casseroles of *Boeuf à la Provençale* thick with a sauce of garlic and anchovies, and the tempting almond and butter aromas of pastries straight out of a gourmand's wildest dreams.

No one seemed to mind the jostling, the storms of confetti, the children racing after lost balloons, or the thundering din of a volunteer band imported from nearby Roberval. Most of the twelve-odd musicians mounted on the temporary bandstand were equiped with violins, flutes, or drums, and they had repeated the farandole from Bizet's *L'Arle'sienne Suite* three times before Terry and Armand had completed their walk around the square. But whatever was lacking in orchestration and repertoire was easily made up in enthusiasm and volume.

A genuine and infectious carnival spirit prevailed — encouraged, at least in part, by free-flowing muscat wine; two tiny cafés, at opposite corners facing the plaza, spilled their customers into the street, where dozens of small tables had been set up for the occasion. Here, local fisherfolk and their neighbors from Roberval mingled amiably with chic vacationers from the capital, members of the American expatriate colony, a few giddy and bejeweled representatives of the elite international set who had raced up from Nice in the vain hope that peasant atmosphere would alleviate their boredom, and a motley assortment of merry tourists, who contributed more color and quaintness than they observed.

A carousel had been set up in a sandy lot near the plaza, and intermittently the caliope sound rose above the band and the cries of *"Bugnes!" "Pan bagna!"* and *"Fleurs de Praline!"* from the food vendors. Over glasses of white wine at one of the lamp-lighted outdoor tables, Armand sang along with the caliope.

*"J'ai perdu le do de
ma Cla-ri-net-te,
J'ai perdu le do de
ma Cla-ri-net-te."*

He interrupted himself to laugh. "I wish that your gardener would lose more than the *'do'* on his flute. Poor Jean-Pierre had no ear for the music. Still — he is an old man, and his more talented friends in the band must tolerate him."

"Jean-Pierre?" Terry craned her neck, but the band was not visible from their table. "Well! Now I feel right at home. I know someone in the band."

"You would not feel, as you say, 'right at home' otherwise?" Armand asked. He re-filled her wineglass from a bottle on the table. "*Blanc de Cassis.* This will make you not think of yourself as a stranger." He shrugged. "Now that you are with us, can we permit for you to feel not welcome?"

"You've done more than your share to make me feel welcome, Armand." Terry indicated the festivities surrounding them with a tilt of her chin. "I'd have missed this . . . I wouldn't have seen anything of the Cote d' Azur if it hadn't been for you."

"You tell me this as if you were to go away tomorrow." Armand's half smile was mourn-ful as he stared into his glass. "We are now friends, is it not so? Not more, not less. As friends, why cannot we enjoy many more . . ."

"I'm leaving Monday," Terry said quietly. "I'm going home."

She might have expected any of a dozen different reactions from Armand: surprise, disappointment, or outrage would have been the most likely bets. Instead, he narrowed his eyes, stared at her accusingly for a few wordless seconds, and then said, "Aha! When I meet you, it is my belief that you intend to win the proposal from Monsieur Olnair, the elder. Now, you fail to win the old millionaire, and you take what is left. The one who will someday be a millionaire. You would not consider to marry a poor village *médecin. Non,* you think of money! Money, money, not one thing more!"

"What did you say?"

Armand was waving his hands wildly for emphasis now. "You think I do not have the good ears? I am like Jean-Pierre? I do not hear what I hear? The younger one — what do you call him? Teek? When I come to the door, he is with his father. They are angry . . . so very angry! And the papa, he cries, 'You know nothing about Terry! Go! Go, if this is what you want to do.' " Armand stopped for a moment to calm himself. "So! Now it is plain. You are going back to America with that . . . that . . ." He made an exaggerated shuddering motion — then tossed off the remainder of his wine. "I do not have the words to tell you what I think of this Teek. Or for what you are going to do."

"All I'm going to do is quit my job!" Terry

protested. "Look, if Mr. Olner and his son were arguing about me, it was probably because Tick can't stand me and his father wants to marry me."

"The *papa* wishes to . . ."

"Yes! You've got it all backwards, Armand. I'm leaving because Richard Olner's already proposed marriage, and I'm not interested. And if Tick is leaving . . . something I didn't know until just now . . . I couldn't care less."

Armand's expression softened, but he was still not completely convinced. "You are both going back? . . ."

"To a big country, my friend. We'll be separated by roughly three thousand miles, about two hundred million other people, and a very strong distaste for each other."

"This is all exactly so?" Armand was hesitant.

Terry examined the cautiously hopeful expression. "I know I was rude to you, Armand, but you can't hate me enough to believe I'd run off with Tick Olner. What can you possibly think of me, if you'd jump to a conclusion like that?"

"I did not wish to think," Armand said. "I must be guided by evidence, *non?* You appear to be greatly in love with romance. All Frenchmen are romantic, and what fool would not wish to live in France? Especially in this so beautiful place? But, from me, and from the Riviera, you wish to escape. What can a man conclude?"

Terry didn't mention the alternative, that she was in love with someone else. Nor did it occur to Armand, though he persisted in his bewildered "analysis" of Terry until a sudden gust of wind, followed by an equally unexpected sprinkle of rain, sent them indoors.

For a while, the outdoor merrymaking continued, probably on the theory that the clouds would go away as abruptly as they had appeared. As Terry and Armand watched from a postage-stamp-sized table near the café's open door, it became apparent that the annual fisherman's fête was going to be rained out.

Even more disconcerting was the wind. Food vendors, the band, everyone concerned with the event made a brave attempt to ignore the storm, but, as paper decorations were ripped from the booths and lanterns swayed crazily before the onshore blow, group after group of local residents and friends from Roberval scurried from the plaza. Not until then did the band give up its resolute tootling and pounding, or the booth operators begin to pack up their crepe pans, soup tureens, and pastry trays

126

for the disheartening trek homeward.

"Oh, it's such a shame!" Terry mourned. "To look forward to an event all year, to make all those preparations, and then . . ."

"*C'est la vie,*" Armand said. "Everyone will make the most of it. Nothing new can be said about this festival . . . it has been going on without change, faithful to every tradition, for hundreds of years. Ah! But this entire year, the folk will wring miles and miles of conversation from the debacle that occurs now. You comprehend, Terry? In a place where so little comes to happen —*voila!* What a remarkable thing there is for to discuss!"

If the local peasantry had retired to their homes to talk about the event, the foreigners and a number of intrepid wine-tipplers from the village seemed determined to keep the carnival spirit alive. As the wind increased, slamming sheets of rain against the café's windows, the door was closed, only to be opened repeatedly, admitting parties of people whose clothes might be damp, but whose determination to have fun was not. The humble café, packed with more people than its owner had probably served in a lifetime, was converted into an impromptu nightclub in which American dowagers rubbed elbows, literally, with fishnetmenders. Its old entrepreneur, quick to recognize a gift from heaven, made frantic dashes in and out of the back door, returning with emergency food supplies; there seemed to be no concern that the mammoth wine barrels would run dry. In the quaint old-world surroundings, the jazz blaring from a flashy jukebox had an anachronistic sound. In a matter of minutes, a noisy party was in full swing.

Terry hadn't seen Bill Lindley come in; perhaps he and the American group with him had squeezed in via the kitchen door. When she did spot him on the dance floor, he was halfheartedly going through the motions of learning a new American dance step from Wanda. As the rock and roll record thumped to a stop, followed by a scratchy Viennese waltz, Terry saw Wanda shove her way to the bar with a stranger. Bill was lost in the crowd for a few moments, and it was Armand who pointed him out next.

"It would seem that everyone is here. The lady who is now dancing with the *docteur* Lindley — you are acquainted, *oui?*"

Terry surveyed Bill's partner for a moment — an elegant and attractive woman who looked familiar. "I . . . think she was on the ship coming over. She's a psychologist."

"Very chic, *non?*" Armand observed. "You see how I am not completely in error about my judgment of romance."

"Your . . . what?"

Armand laughed. "You are not listening to me." Speaking in a tone that competed with the clamor of voices, the music, the strident shriek of the wind and the waterfall effect of rain on the tiled roof, he explained. "I have not yet made a conclusion about you, Terry. But with the *médecin,* it is most simple to see. The young girl . . . what do they call her?"

"Wanda?"

"*Oui.* Mademoiselle Olnair. I watch her make the fool of herself. She would, as one might say, jump through the hoop to have the attention of the *médecin.*" Armand shrugged. "He could not possibly to fall for someone so shallow, so . . . obvious. But the lady who is with him now! . . ." Armand bunched his fingers and kissed the tips. "She has, as you can see, all that a man of quality would desire. Beauty, intelligence, a quiet dignity even in a not so dignified scene as this." He was watching the couple with a satisfied glow in his eyes, as though he had personally arranged the match. "Observe how they dance, Terry. One who is so expert in the matter of romance as Gautier can say with no hesitation . . . there are two people in love!"

Armand's observations in that area had been 100 percent wrong, Terry reminded herself. The reminder was futile. Tears welled up in her eyes, and turning her face to pretend interest in an incongruous pair of waltzing hippies near the door only called Armand's attention to the fact. She heard the romance expert inhale a long breath, audible in spite of the din assaulting her ears.

Terry managed to blink away the tears, sniffing deliberately, blotting her eyes with a paper napkin. "I must . . . be catching cold," she said. "This damp air . . . so much smoke in here . . ."

Armand pronounced his words like a prosecuting attorney throwing out a clinching statement. "You are in love with him! With *le docteur* Lindley, you are madly in love!"

Terry's silence was the only acknowledgment Armand required. "Incredible! And he does not know! *Sacré bleu,* you Americans, how *naïve!*" Armand drew himself up in something like a nationalistic, military position. "A French woman would not sit here with tears in her eyes. She would fight. You deserve to lose this man, you are no more strong than . . . what? The meringue. Soft. Poof! Nothing but air."

Before Terry lost control of her tears, Armand changed his strategy from challenge to Dutch-uncle advice. He seemed to have eliminated himself as a contender with no serious emotional disturbance. He was confidential and objective as he raked up one hoary platitude after another, giving Terry suggestions that would have sounded insipid in an advice-to-the-lovelorn column at the turn of the century. Still, there was no doubting the young doctor's sincerity; perhaps the old tried-and-true approaches to love were still valid, but only if you were French.

Fortunately, Armand's interest did not confine itself to words. Somehow, in spite of the crowd, he maneuvered Terry out onto the dance floor. With equal aplomb, he steered her toward Bill Lindley and his arresting partner. There was a brief exchange; there were introductions — and then, in the smoothest and most overwhelming operation since D-day, Terry discovered herself dancing with the man she loved.

A sentimental, currently popular French ballad was pouring from the jukebox now. It was relaxing music that, in combination with the wine, helped Terry overcome her stiffness in Bill's arms. Nor was there any need to search for fascinating things to say; the hilarity of the crowd had risen in proportion to the intensity of the storm outside. Terry closed her eyes, letting her head rest lightly against Bill's shoulder, letting the dream and the music and the wine carry her.

She was barely aware of the record ending, and another beginning; this time a honky-tonk American number dating back to the twenties. Its bouncy rhythm shot a renewed wave of animation into the crowd, and a bearded, barefoot artist-type from St. Tropez, shirt emblazoned with psychedelic patterns, swung by with an overdressed matron from the mink coat set. "Man, this is so square it's hip again!"

Bill laughed and pressed Terry closer in an effort to protect her from another pair who had decided to revive the Watusi in time to a vaudeville-age beat.

"I wouldn't have missed this for all the plush spots on the coast," Bill said. "Laura ought to be taking notes."

Terry forced down the wave of jealousy that had swept over her. "Is Dr. Congreve . . . a clinical psychologist?"

"No, Laura's giving up a private practice to do behavioral research for a book."

Terry felt suddenly small and insignificant. She heard herself making the most inane comment possible. "Oh, she's going to write a book?"

It took several seconds before Bill's reply registered in her mind. "No, her fiancé's writing it. He's a psychiatrist with a practice in Rome. Laura came over to help him with statistics, and, just incidentally, to marry the guy." Bill glanced toward the bar and grinned. "I hope he's going to write his book. He won't, if Laura doesn't get him away from his personal research project tonight. We were all kidding him last week about being a teetotaler. You see, Dr. Rinaldi's recognized as an authority on alcoholism, and he doesn't drink. So tonight he said he's going to test the effects of St. Juste grape juice . . . in the interest of science."

Terry had been listening to the joking recital with only half an ear. She was only aware that Bill was talking about two casual friends who were engaged to be married — talking as though it was assumed that he had come to the village celebration with a party of professional people he had met in Nice. They were shipboard and resort acquaintances — the sort of people you enjoyed during a vacation and promptly forgot about when the holiday ended. Was the fact that Bill Lindley hadn't appeared with a date a reason to feel encouraged? Or did it simply mean that he hadn't yet stopped mourning the one great tragic love in his life — that his carefree attitude was only a temporary escape, a façade behind which that old grief still tormented him?

Terry dismissed the question from her mind. All that mattered now was savoring the moment. She was doing exactly that when Bill said, "I wonder what's going on?"

Terry raised her head. "Why do you ask, Bill?"

"I don't know. Look."

Most of the people around them had stopped dancing and were moving toward the kitchen. A curious hush had fallen over the room; the voices were subdued now, and it seemed to Terry that questions ran through the restrained hubbub. She looked around for Armand, but he was nowhere in sight. Bill, meanwhile, had asked the young American in the wildly colored shirt what was wrong.

"I'm not sure," Bill was told. "Something about a ship breaking up on the rocks offshore. Some cat came in with the news a minute ago — I guess looking for a couple of local guys who own boats. A couple of them just tore out the back door."

"You mean it's happening now?" Terry asked.

The bearded youth looked past her with an abstracted expression. "Man, everything that's happening is happening now!"

They looked for more logical sources for answers. A doll-like girl Terry had seen wearing a nurse's uniform at the clinic in Roberval was slipping a sweater over her shoulders. Without looking at Bill, she said, "Yes, they say is very bad. Maybe they . . . save some peoples, they will be hurt. So I go see."

"Do you need . . . would you like a ride to the hospital?" Bill offered.

"Oh, no," the nurse replied. She was on her way to the less crowded area around the front door. "I think better I go to the beach. *Le docteur* Gautier, he . . . want this, to help him."

A few hardy souls, more curious than cautious, were already running toward the quay. Others, avoiding the rain, remained inside the smoke-filled café exchanging conjecture about the shipwreck.

"Dr. Gautier may need all the help he can get," Bill said. They had followed the clinic nurse as if by blind instinct. Now, at the open doorway, Bill hesitated as a blast of windblown water hurled itself at them. Over

135

the noise of the storm, he shouted, "I don't know whether I'll be ruder if I ask you to stay here or if I ask you to come along, Terry."

"I don't have to be asked," Terry yelled back.

Heads down against the wind, they raced toward the beach.

CHAPTER 10

Flickering oil lamps created rings of yellow light on the wet sand, lending an eerie nightmare quality to the shadow figures that raced back and forth.

Within the past ten minutes the wind had decreased and the deluge of water from the sky had thinned to a soft, steady rain. But the churning surf, stirred up by the treacherous gregale, had not lessened its fury. Its roar drowned out all but the loudest cries; fishermen barking terse orders to each other as they struggled to retrieve a small boat, overturned in the launching, and now flopping insanely near the sand.

Groups of awed spectators stood huddled along the shoreline, their eyes riveted on three specks of moving light that shimmered, disappeared from view, and emerged again above the wild black water like twinkling stars. The lanterns aboard those three wave-tossed boats beamed a final ray of hope for sailors still believed to be clinging to a stretch of barnacle-crusted rocks some five hundred yards offshore. At rhythmic intervals the warning beacon posted on this rugged outcropping (usually a perch for gulls) turned to give the beach a fleeting glimpse of the shattering hull of a white freighter. It lay on its side like a dead whale, passively pulled back from the reef only to be rammed against it once again. It was impossible to distinguish between the sound of the sea and the splintering of that massive vessel in its death agony.

Armand had made every preliminary arrangement possible. The clinic had been contacted and instructed to be ready for possible survivors. Roberval's single ambulance was on its way to the scene, and the carnival committee had applied itself to the grimmer task of organizing transportation to the clinic, five miles inland.

"We have notified the Red Cross in Nice," Armand said. He had come to stand beside Bill Lindley, Terry, and the petite nurse from his clinic, who had introduced herself as Mireille Lavour. Unmindful of their dripping clothes, the quartet waited, as helpless as the others who kept vigil on the beach. Armand raised his voice, uncertain whether he had been heard. "I prepare for many who

138

survive," he shouted. "Not to do so is to lose the faith, *non?*"

The others agreed. No one could bear to voice the almost certain belief that medical help would not be needed. One needed only to look out toward the flashing beacon, to catch glimpses of that agitated sea rising to pound the reef, and it became clear that survivors would constitute a miracle.

They watched the bobbing lights of the rescue boats — and waited. At times one of the lantern lights was swallowed in darkness for a seeming eternity. When the light reappeared there was a collective sigh of relief before tension gripped the watchers once again.

"To go out into that deliberately . . ." Bill's words were lost in the thunder of the surf, but Terry understood what he meant. The sailors aboard that freighter had been given no choice; but the fishermen of St. Juste had plunged their boats into the sea voluntarily and without hesitation. Their courage was reflected by the villagers who lined the shore. No one questioned the logic of risking death in the slim hope that total strangers might still be alive on those rocks. Friends and relatives traced the perilous course of the tiny boats with their eyes — and were silent.

Terry saw Armand walk toward a lone figure standing several yards down the beach. Through the rain, she made out the lantern-lighted features of Jean-Pierre, Olner's gardener and bane of the local band. Armand stood beside the man for several minutes, speaking to him. After a while, the doctor patted the old man's shoulder and returned to his former place. "In the first boat," Armand yelled by way of explanation. "The two young men, they are the sons of Jean-Pierre."

"Oh, Mon Dieu, Mon Dieu!" Mireille cried. She had said almost nothing until then. Now the pretty little brunette shook her head sorrowfully. *"S'ils étaient mes fils, je ne les laisserais pas partir!"*

Armand turned to Terry. "Mireille says to me if they were her sons, she would not let them go. But this is not so. She is from the village. A nurse, she thinks only of saving the lives." Although the words were shouted, they sounded soft and tender. "Who can say what Mireille would do if she had sons to love, *hein?*"

The girl's English was too scanty, Terry was certain, to understand what had been said. But in the pale light, Mireille's dark eyes turned momentarily from the sea to Armand's face. Under less anguished circumstances, Terry would have smiled. Apparently Dr. Gautier, the expert in romantic matters, was unable to recognize love even when it was beamed directly at him.

That swift impression occupied Terry's thoughts for no more than a few seconds. It was the only distraction in what became an almost unbearable period of suspense. And then someone was pointing out to sea and shouting, *"Ils reviennent!"*

"They're coming back," Bill echoed.

Terry followed the lights as they moved shoreward now. The danger was not over, but every moment that passed brought the barely discernible boats closer and closer to safety. They rode low in the water, sunk almost to their gunwales by heavy weight. It was Jean-Pierre who cried, *"Ils sont sains et saufs!"*

An intense excitement seized the watchers as the silhouetted forms in one boat, then another, and another came into view.

"They've got others with them!" Bill pointed out.

A group of men waded out as far as the surf permitted, ready to pull in the first returning boat.

Minutes later, the beach resembled an international first-aid station, with Armand Gautier in charge. His problems were compounded by a language barrier; the sailors, a number of them seriously injured, were Burmese. One man, whose skin had been scraped raw by barnacles as the waves grated his body back and forth over the rocks, had also sustained a more serious head injury; unlike the uniformly dressed sailors, he wore a business suit, wet and shredded now. Someone said he was a Chinese passenger en route to Marseilles from Hong Kong. As Terry bent over the man to give him emergency treatment, before his transfer to a Citroen station wagon, the man kept muttering, *"Yīshēng . . . yīshēng."* Apparently the word meant "doctor," for when Bill took charge, the man appeared satisfied that the proper things were being done for him and promptly lapsed into unconsciousness.

Most of the work involved first aid and supervising the movement of patients to waiting cars. Terry worked under Bill Lindley's guidance. He, in turn, recognized Armand Gautier as his superior; it was the latter who expedited the removal of the most severely injured survivors first. He left the scene with the last of these — a Burmese sailor whose leg had been crushed when the cargo of teakwood became dislodged. "I will take the young man to Roberval myself,"

Armand said. He was breathless, but completely in control of the situation. "*Merci beaucoup* for all you have done, *docteur* . . . and you, Terry."

"I know we aren't licensed to practice here," Bill told him as Armand got behind the wheel of his car. Mireille was doing her best to make the patient comfortable in the back seat. "I don't want to imply that your clinic isn't prepared . . ."

"We are not prepared with all the personnel we would wish," Armand said. "Not for so great a disaster. There are twenty-six who will need care. If we could have two surgeries in operation at once . . ."

"We'll follow you," Bill said. There was no more discussion of the law prohibiting a foreign doctor to operate in Roberval's small hospital. Two local men had sustained injuries in the rescue attempt; not one of the Burmese had escaped shock.

Following Armand's car, Bill turned briefly to address Terry. "One of the sailors spoke a little English. You remember the chap with the dislocated shoulder . . . the one Jean-Pierre's son carried onto the beach?"

"Yes. He was extremely feverish, Bill. As though he'd been ill before the ship was wrecked."

143

"That's the man. He was delirious. Do you know how many there were aboard, Terry? Forty-two crewmen and eight passengers."

Terry shuddered. "I don't suppose there's . . . any hope for the others?"

Bill shook his head gravely. "What an ending for the town's big celebration. Tomorrow they'll be patrolling the beach, looking for bodies."

Wet and cold, they drove most of the way to the neighboring village without speaking, each absorbed in a private review of the tragedy. There was little to say in the wake of that awesome scene on the beach.

At the clinic, too, they said little because there was no time for idle conversation.

Through one of the freighter's rescued passengers, a French student, they got a graphic picture of the horror that had been invisible from the beach. The storm had risen in full fury without warning. The first blow had sent timber flying in the hold; few of the crewmen below deck had escaped. Others, as the ship was slammed against the reef, were hit by flying debris. Only a small percentage reached the precarious safety of the rocks, and even there they were pummeled not only by the sea but by the wreckage of the ship itself.

For the medical team, the result was a demanding variety of injuries, the least of which were deep, salt-irritated abrasions.

It was exhausting and depressing, yet the experience held within it a moment of truth for Terry. Near sunrise, when Armand gave his grateful assurance that there was nothing more for the American doctor and nurse to do, and as medical reinforcements began to arrive from other areas, Terry stopped to tell Mireille that she would return the borrowed uniform the next day.

In the nurses' dressing room, where Mireille sipped black coffee and repeated Armand's thanks for the help, Terry dropped her ruined blue silk dress into a waste container, then carefully removed the French nurses' cap, with its traditional red cross and veil. "I should thank you, Mireille, for letting me wear this."

The girl smiled wanly. "It make one so proud, *oui?*"

"Any nurse's cap does that," Terry said. "But sometimes you take it for granted. You forget the responsibilities . . . the purpose. Do you understand what I mean?"

Mireille blushed. "I . . . think no. My English . . . I try to learn . . . because *le docteur* Gautier . . . he will like if I know something. You know? . . . ." The blush

145

deepened as Mireille groped for words that eluded her. Still, she could not have expressed more clearly that she tried to improve her education in the hope of attracting a young doctor from Paris whose comparative sophistication awed her. "You were say . . . about the . . ."

"The cap. The uniform." Terry released a long sigh. "I haven't been a credit to it lately, Mireille. I've only been pretending I'm a nurse, to pamper a patient who no longer needs me. Tonight I . . . realized how . . . how much I really *am* needed. Here, at home . . . somewhere, there's always someone who desperately needs a nurse." For a few seconds, Terry stood still, running her fingers across the starched edge of the cap. "Don't ever let yourself forget that, Mireille. You're important. Don't let anyone sidetrack you from your purpose in wearing that cap."

In spite of her weariness, Mireille laughed. "Here, mademoiselle, *le docteur* do not give me . . . one minutes to forgot."

Impulsively, Terry gave the tiny girl a brief hug. "Someone had better remind him of a few other things," she said. She said goodnight to Mireille, leaving Armand's undiscovered gem staring at her in total bewilderment.

There was no rain as Bill Lindley steered the Peugeot back to the villa at St. Juste. A pale-pink blush was rising in the east, and the day promised to be as clear and lovely as only days in the south of France can be. Events of the night before belonged to some distorted dream. Terry's body felt a weariness beyond belief, but every nerve was keyed up with awareness of the man beside her; her vicarious pride in his swift judgments on the beach and at the clinic, his calm patience with the terrified and shocked young sailors from Burma (most of them had seemed to be no more than teen-agers) and the humility with which he had accepted Armand's thanks.

So much that she wanted to say to Bill! Yet, when she finally spoke, Terry came out with a tired inanity. "It was so horrible. I wish it hadn't happened, but . . . I'm glad we were here."

"I'm glad we were here, too," Bill said.

No doubt he was more completely enervated than Terry. This was why he drove steadily and quietly the rest of the way home, she told herself. It was hardly the setting for more promising words, and she was almost too tired for disappointment when Bill left her at her door with no more than a whispered goodnight.

147

CHAPTER 11

Terry awoke as a bright beam of sunlight struck her face. She turned her head on the pillow and opened her eyes to see Irene Washburn pulling the heavy draperies aside.

"Almost noon," Irene said. "I hated to get you outta the sack, kid, but Doc Lindley wants to see you."

Terry was instantly awake. "What about? Did he say?" The nightmare of the preceding hours flooded over her, unbelievable, and yet disturbingly real.

"I dunno. He talked to Dr. What's-His-Name on the phone a little while ago."

"Gautier?" Terry slid out of bed and started for the bathroom.

"Yeah. He's all shook up about somethin' . . . don't ask me what."

While Terry splashed cold water on her face, Irene talked to her from the bedroom. "That was sure awful, what happened last night. I wouldn't have wanted to be out in

148

that water — boy, I had the willies right here, tryin' to keep Mr. O. an' Junior from flippin' their wigs."

Terry blotted her face hurriedly with a towel. "You what?"

"They was in a regular swivet, with all that wind. Up here, it sounded like the whole joint was gonna blow over the cliff. See, one thing I know about this family, honey — they scare awful easy. Me an' Carl, we was in a million storms . . . on a carny lot, when a big blow hits, you're so busy holdin' the gear together, you ain't got the time to get scared; but you take people that like everything nice an' comfy all the time, they panic. Carl just about took another swing at Tick, the kid got so hy-sterical." Charitably, Irene acknowledged that Richard Olner's illness had probably contributed to his nervous state. "He was actually beefin' that you an' Doc Lindley wasn't here. Like a nurse an' a doctor could push a button an' stop the wind from blowin'."

While Terry dressed, Irene gave her a second-hand account of activities in St. Juste. She eliminated no gruesome detail and probably embellished a few from her imagination. "It's awful. Just awful . . . all them poor people drowned like that. That guy that takes care of the yard . . . you know the old geezer with the name you spell like a girl's . . ."

"Jean-Pierre?"

"Yeah. He showed up late — about ten o'clock — an' then he left right away. Just come up to tell Carl he couldn't work today, on accounta he was to help down at the beach. The old guy was actually bawlin', Carl told me. Him an' Carl talk in sign language, but he got it across that his two boys was heroes." Irene paused. "That's how people are. Somethin' happens, they wanna get a little glory out of it. Not that I blame . . ."

"His sons brought eight people back off that rock," Terry said. "In a boat that was probably meant for four people, all told."

"No kiddin'! They really made like heroes, huh? You seen the whole thing?"

Terry daubed on a touch of lipstick. "I'll tell you about it later — I'd better see what's happening." She thanked Irene for coming up to waken her, and was on her way down the stairs in a matter of seconds.

Bill got out of his chair as Terry hurried into the dining room. Richard was at the table, too, looking almost as wrung out as some of the survivors Terry had tended the night before.

There was a brief exchange of good mornings. Terry sat down, Bill resumed his seat, and a maid appeared with orange juice, fresh coffee, and sweet rolls. While she laid out a table setting for Terry, Bill said, "I didn't like having to disturb you, Terry, but Dr. Gautier phoned with a problem."

"I still can't see that it's . . . Terry's problem," Richard grumbled. "Nor, for that matter . . . yours, Bill. These people have their . . . own medical services. You said yourself they . . . do an efficient job. You're here on a . . . vacation and, besides, you . . . can get yourself into a peck of trouble with . . . the government if you . . . so much as look at a patient here. I don't blame you for . . . pitching in during an emergency, like . . . last night. But you're . . . sticking your neck out if . . . ."

"Richard!" Bill had listened to the irritable lecture patiently, but apparently his patience had run out. "This is a professional request, and it doesn't involve actual medical services."

"I wish you'd tell me what Dr. Gautier called about," Terry protested.

Richard drummed his fingers on the table, obviously annoyed.

"Do you recall the young man we discussed on the way to the clinic last night, Terry?" Bill paused for an instant. "You commented on his feverish appearance."

"Oh, yes . . . the one Jean-Pierre's older boy carried in. The one who spoke some English?"

"That's the man. You were right about the fever. I didn't see him at the hospital, but Gautier's had him under close observation. This morning he diagnosed the poor devil's condition as smallpox."

Terry drew a sharp, involuntary breath. "Oh, Bill!"

"Gautier has public health authorities here . . . they've already clamped a quarantine on Roberval and St. Juste. You can imagine what would happen if someone who'd had contact with the man took off for Nice this morning . . . or Paris. Anywhere. Someone who might not be vaccinated."

"No chance of you contacting the disease?" Richard asked. He appeared queasy, looking from Bill to Terry apprehensively. "You took . . . care of this fellow . . . touched him?"

Bill sighed his exasperation. Evidently he had been asked the question before. "I told you, Richard, nobody who travels has to worry about smallpox. You can't get a passport . . . in fact, you couldn't get back into the United States without an up-to-date World Health Organization card. I took care of the cards myself, for all of us."

"Then what's all the fuss about?" Richard demanded. Terry had never seen him this surly before, and his resentment seemed to include her. "I might point out that . . . Terry is a . . . private nurse. *My* nurse."

Richard's accent on the possessive pronoun rankled inside Terry, but she ignored the speech. It was typical of Richard to think of people who worked for him as property. When he said, "my doctor," or "my attorney," or "my broker," there was always this indication of ownership. No one was going to change his attitude, and what difference would it make after Monday? Fleetingly, Terry remembered that she hadn't yet told Richard she was leaving. For that matter, Bill hadn't been told, either. What difference did it make?

". . . that no one's trying to hijack your private nurse," Bill was saying. His tone was extremely calm, but his irritation, Terry suspected, was as great as Richard's. "All Dr. Gautier wants of us is a little help with a routine check-up in St. Juste. We'll remember the people who actually had contact with the patient. Jean-Pierre's son, for example. And, from there we'll have to make certain that everyone he's contacted has been inoculated against smallpox."

"That could be the . . . whole damned village!" Richard exploded. "Everybody knows everybody, down there. They're probably getting together to discuss the thing . . . all of them down at the beach or jammed into the town saloon . . ."

"That's exactly why we want to give these people all the cooperation we can," Bill said. "It's a routine matter, actually, but Gautier has his hands full at the clinic. Anyway, he thinks medical people who've had contact with the patient will have a good psychological effect. Reassure people. Let them know there's no reason for concern, unless they haven't been vaccinated. The public health people may even order revaccinations for everyone in the village. That's the procedure during epidemics. And we've got to remember that all of this patient's shipmates were exposed."

"How are you going to . . . reassure anybody when you don't even speak the . . . language?" Richard cried. His agitation seemed entirely out of proportion with the simple plan they were discussing. "All right, you'll have those . . . health people to . . . translate. It's still a . . . risky proposition."

Why should Richard be so upset? Terry wondered. He had made few demands upon her time lately. He certainly couldn't feel any jealousy toward Bill Lindley. Why, then, was he objecting to this perfectly reasonable request from the man who would soon be his personal physician? What was "risky" about it?

Bill asked the last question aloud, though he phrased it more subtly. "Are you concerned about something you haven't told me about, Richard?"

"Maybe I am! How do we know this . . . Burmese fellow has . . . smallpox? I'm no doctor, but I know . . . the disease is almost . . . extinct. How do we know he doesn't have . . . something a lot worse? Something . . . very contagious?"

Bill looked puzzled. "I know it because I have every reason to respect Dr. Gautier's opinion. Look, Richard, I'll grant you the disease is no longer common — not even in the most underdeveloped areas. But it's by no means extinct. I'm sure Gautier's diagnosis is correct."

"Doesn't it occur to you that . . . he's lying?"

Richard's shrill accusation crackled through the room. Bill glanced at Terry, frowned, and then said quietly. "That's a serious charge, Richard. Apart from the fact that it wouldn't make sense for one doctor to lie to another. For what possible reason?"

"To prevent a panic! Keep you here to . . . 'reassure' people. *Use* you. They have all those . . . terrible diseases in the eastern countries . . . same as Africa. Terrible diseases. Listen! You can go out among those people, Bill, but . . . don't come back here . . . contaminate the place before we get out."

"Get out? Richard, you can't be serious!"

"We're driving to Marseilles. Soon as I get the . . . Washburns to pack our things." Richard got up from the table, his legs trembling under him. As Terry moved to give him support, he sank back into his chair, an expression of undisguised terror in his eyes. "We're getting out of here!" he shouted.

"You can't leave," Bill said. He spoke as though he were addressing a frightened child, "I told you the area's been quarantined, but that's no reason for you to panic." He reached across the table to pat Richard's forearm. "Take it easy, friend. There's absolutely no cause for alarm. Matter of fact, the only danger you're risking is getting yourself into a swivet. Just take my word for it and relax. Terry and I will give the folks down below a hand, and that's all there'll be to it."

Richard Olner's reaction was a shocking

156

one; the man who had impressed everyone with his courageous battle against paralysis covered his face with his hands. "I've had enough! I'm still young . . . I have things to do! My business!" His voice was reduced to a fearful whimper. "I came here to . . . get my strength back. I didn't . . . come here to die of some loathsome sickness."

Bill was obviously touched, but he remained firm. "Richard, I don't know what you've imagined here. Surely you know you can trust me to . . ."

The sentence was cut off abruptly as Carl Washburn came into the room. "S'cuse me, Mr. O. . . . your daughter says Irene should pack up everything an' I should get the cars ready. We goin' somewheres?"

Before Richard could answer, Wanda pushed her way past the chauffeur. "Will you get a move on, Carl? When I tell you to do something, don't waste time checking on my orders. Get going!"

Carl ignored the girl, looking to Richard for advice. "Is that right, Boss? It seems kinda . . ."

"Do as she says," Richard croaked. He took his hands from his face and addressed an appeal to Terry. "Come with us, dear. I don't want anything . . . to happen to you."

Bill leaped out of his chair. "What *is* this?

You aren't making sense."

"You're the one who's not making sense!" Wanda shrieked. "You call yourself a doctor! And she . . . that man-chasing tramp calls herself a nurse! You're too stupid to know what's really going on! You shouldn't be here . . . I don't even want to get near you!"

Terry listened to the mounting hysteria, dumbfounded. For an instant her eyes met Bill's; he was equally stunned by the outburst.

"I was . . . going to ask you about it," Richard said. "Then you . . . got that call from Gautier and . . . I knew. You doctors . . . you always stick together . . . trying to avoid a panic."

"You'd let us die," Wanda cried, "rather than admit you don't know bubonic plague when you see it!"

For a few seconds, Terry thought Bill was going to break out in laughter. Sensibly, recognizing genuine fear, he said, "Wanda, that's the most absurd thing I've ever heard. You're talking about one man with a curable illness. We're all immunized against smallpox. There's no question of a plague!"

Even Carl Washburn looked uneasy now. "She talked to that Jean-Pierre this morning. Maybe he knew somethin' we don't know, Doc."

"Jean-Pierre is a simple, probably superstitious peasant," Bill argued. "What did he actually say?"

"Plague!" Wanda backed away toward the door as Bill moved toward her. "Don't get near me! You touched that man. You both did. Dad, get away from them! It spreads so fast — it can wipe out thousands of people in . . ."

"Will you stop and think?" Bill ordered. "Plague. In a peasant's vocabulary, that could apply to any contagious disease. Didn't he say *'la variole'?* That's smallpox. He was probably remembering that before the cowpox injection was developed, smallpox decimated whole populations. Not only in Europe, Wanda. Millions of Indians died when the white men carried the virus into the Americas."

Richard Olner had pulled himself up to his feet, Carl jumping forward to guide him toward the door. Wanda's reminder of contamination had suddenly, absurdly, made him fearful of contact with either his doctor or Terry. It was totally incongruous; a moment ago he had been pleading with Terry to "escape" with him. Now he was avoiding her like . . . like the *plague!*

"You don't understand the language," Bill

was saying reasonably. "I'm sure you misunderstood the man, Wanda. In any case, he's probably confused about what he heard. Silly rumors . . ."

"Tick heard him, too," Wanda said. "Jean-Pierre didn't say anything about *la . . .* whatever you said. *'La peste'*, that's the other word he used. Tick looked it up in the dictionary. It means plague!"

"Shut up and let's get going!" Terry looked past the other Olners to see Tick outside the open doorway. He sounded more terrified, if that was possible, than his sister. "Forget the packing. The maids skipped . . . they know what's going on. Leave the junk here and let's cut."

"It's a serious breach of the law to break quarantine." Bill must have realized that an appeal to Tick's reason was hopeless. He turned to Richard. "Wait a minute. Think! You'll be stopped anyway, Richard. The excitement's going to be too much for you."

"We're getting out of here if we have to shoot our way out," Tick yelled back. He was halfway across the small salon, on his way to the front door. "Come on, Washburn! Get Dad into the car!"

The telephone in the vestibule rang, but no one moved to answer it. It continued its shrill summons intermittently, ignored.

"Richard, this is insane," Bill was pleading. "If there was any truth to the rumor, do you think I'd lie to you? I'm your doctor . . . your friend. Terry's the girl you're going to marry. Have you gone mad?"

No one replied. Hastily, head downcast, Richard allowed himself to be led out of the dining room.

Terry started after her patient. "He doesn't know what he's doing, Bill. Don't let him go like this. The shock is liable to . . ."

"Keep away from us!" Wanda screamed. "You keep away!" She broke into a run, ignoring her father's stumbling progress as she raced for the front door.

Carl turned, shrugging helplessly at Terry. "Me an' Irene will do the best we can, honey."

From outside the house, Wanda screeched, "Irene! Forget the damn luggage and get down here!"

"I'm your doctor, Richard," Bill repeated. It was a final, parting shot, and Bill must have known that it would have no effect. Short of trying to restrain Richard by physical force, an unthinkable procedure, there was nothing he could do to dissuade the millionaire from fleeing the premises. The doctor, like Terry, was probably concluding that Richard's obsession with being strong,

161

healthy, and powerful had contributed to his phenomenal recovery. But the same obsession was now at the root of his mindless fear; Richard Olner had to survive. Nothing and no one else mattered, and in his unreasoning panic Richard had quite forgotten that the man who was advising him not to run was the same physician who had guided him out of a near-vegetable state.

"Forget it," Bill sighed. "They aren't going anywhere, and it's bad medicine to create a scene."

Terry agreed, depending on Irene to apply her blunt reasoning to the situation and to calm the hysteria. "We'd better report to the clinic. The Olners are adults — at least technically. If they want to run and tell the king the sky is falling down, like Chicken Little, we can't stop them."

Bill shook his head back and forth slowly. "It's incredible. And the irony is . . . if that crazy story were true, it wouldn't do them any good to run. Wanda and Tick stood around discussing it with the father of the guy who carried that 'bubonic plague' victim from the boat. First thing Jean-Pierre did was to hug his kid. How's that for passing the plague around?"

"I wouldn't blame an uneducated man

like the gardener for misunderstanding," Terry said. "But Richard!"

A motor roared outside the garage, and then a second car was started up. "At least they're leaving us one of the rented crates," Bill observed. "That'll save walking down to the village."

The ringing telephone, ignored during the frantic exodus, had been silent for a few moments. Now it rang again and Terry walked to the vestibule to answer it. She had barely picked up the receiver and said, "Hello?" when Armand Gautier's voice exploded in her ear.

"Terry? Where have you been? What are you people doing to me? *Mon Dieu,* can you not understand the consequence of what you have done?" Armand was normally excitable, but never as agitated as he sounded now.

"What are you talking about?" Terry asked. "Is something wrong?"

"Here, outside the hospital, are people to demand that I remove the smallpox patient. They have gone mad with fear. Of course I cannot move the man . . . with good care, I have all hopes to make him well."

"People are demanding? . . ."

Terry's question was cut off by a protest that verged on the edge of tears. "In St.

Juste, I am told, people are packing their few possessions and preparing to leave . . . where, God alone can tell. There will not be enough quarantine officers to detain them. It is possible that to escape a plague that is only imagined, one villager or two will carry smallpox to another area. Worse — worse, there may be violence. Why? Why have you permitted this, you and *le docteur?*"

"Please try to calm yourself, Armand. Would you rather talk to . . ."

"*Non, non,* there is no time for talk. You must go to the village. Perhaps if you can make the people believe that I have not deceived them . . . that the American *médecin* has not advised his friends to run away. . . ."

A wave of nausea swept over Terry. "The Olners just left here. They misunderstood something they heard from the gardener. . . ."

Armand groaned. "And he and the other servants have spread the word throughout the village. Even here in Roberval, the people believe I lie to them. They say the Americans would not be leaving if there was not great danger to stay. Mademoiselle, you must do something! . . . Lindley! You must convince *le docteur* . . ."

"He doesn't need convincing," Terry said.

164

"We'll do anything you want us to do."

"Go to the village," Armand instructed. "Mademoiselle Lavour . . . Mireille, she has gone to St. Juste to speak to her people. But she is no more than a child, and she has had no sleep. What can she do?" There was an anguished sigh from Armand; it was obvious that he was near the breaking point from exhaustion. "Who knows — she may turn against me with the rest."

"Hang on," Terry directed. "We're on our way."

Seconds after she had dropped the receiver, Terry was hurrying out of the villa with Bill Lindley at her side. Instinctively, Bill waited until they were on their way to the village before asking for details. As a doctor and a man well read in history, he knew only too well what could happen when an entire community panics in the face of a deadly plague. Perhaps he hurried because he knew, also, that terrified peasants had once fought such pestilence with fire. The patient in Dr. Gautier's clinic represented a threat to lives in Roberval. How long could Armand keep a panic-stricken mob at bay?

By the time they reached the village square, Terry not only knew what she was expected to do; she knew that Bill Lindley was needed more desperately five miles away. Whatever could be done to restore confidence in St. Juste, she would have to do alone.

CHAPTER 12

As Bill Lindley sped off toward the clinic in Roberval, Terry crossed the tiny plaza of St. Juste. The gravel pathway leading to the make-shift bandstand was littered with wet crepe paper streamers and soggy confetti, symbolic reminders of the gaiety that had died there so suddenly the night before.

A group of villagers milled around the platform from which Jean-Pierre had tootled his flatly resolute notes for a happier crowd. Some of the people carried battered suitcases. A number of women guarded priceless treasures — a portable sewing machine, a carton of china bric-a-brac. Around them huddled equally bewildered children; most of the youngsters clutched a favorite pet — one of the mongrel dogs that scoured the quay in search of fish scraps, a kitten . . . even a squawking chicken.

The speaker on the platform, a smartly suited, middle-aged man, was unquestionably an "outsider," probably one of the public health officers or a representative of the Red Cross. His rapid French escaped Terry completely. It seemed to be having little influence on those who understood his words; the local fishermen and their families had started to edge away from the center of the plaza.

If they had no confidence in a countryman who spoke with the calm voice of authority, how could a stranger appeal to them . . . a stranger who knew only a handful of words in French, and inappropriate words at that? The hopelessness of . . .

"Mademoiselle Terry!"

Terry whipped around to see Mireille on the periphery of the crowd. The young nurse's face looked haggard and tear-stained, but she ran toward Terry with a desperate eagerness. "Oh, *mademoiselle,* you are here! My friends . . . they not believe me! They say you go . . . oh, please . . ."

Mireille's cry had interrupted the speaker. His voice drifted off into a startling silence, during which the eyes of the crowd followed his puzzled stare, fixing themselves upon the foreigner who had so rudely disrupted the proceedings.

Terry felt her face coloring, but she remembered Bill's admonition, "Act as

though you didn't have a care in the world."
She nodded respectfully at the speaker and
smiled at Mireille. In almost the same
instant, she noticed Jean-Pierre, a woman
she presumed to be the gardener's wife, and
the two husky young men who had proven
themselves heroes on the preceding night.
"Tell everyone it's all a mistake," she whispered to Mireille. "Get Jean-Pierre to repeat
what he told the Americans on the hill.
They're stupid people — they don't understand your language. They're not like Jean-
Pierre's sons. Mireille, explain to these
people that those hysterical cowards don't
even have sense enough to trust in their own
doctor!"

Mireille hesitated. "I do try! They say . . .
I only tell them stories . . . because I am in
love to Armand Gautier."

"Tell them I'm a nurse and I'm staying
right here. Dr. Lindley's gone to the clinic.
Mireille, I can't speak French. Dr. Gautier
can't count on anyone here except you!"

Mireille's eyes resembled those of the
proverbial frightened doe. Then, darting
around to take in the mingled fear and
hostility, the expectant expressions of people
around her, the little nurse turned toward
Jean-Pierre, asking him a series of rapid-fire
questions, unintelligible to Terry, but of

consummate interest to the crowd. There was a period of hand-waving, head-shaking, shoulder-shrugging and exasperated explaining on Jean-Pierre's part. A few of the villagers who had inched away from the platform now moved in closer, listening with suspicious but hopeful expressions on their faces. The dignified gentleman who had been addressing the group bent down to reach his hand out to Mireille, inviting her to join him on the platform.

Mireille hesitated, her fright almost palpable now.

It didn't take much imagination to understand and even to empathize with the young nurse's apprehension. Basically shy and reserved, probably terrified of standing up and speaking before a crowd, Mireille was also aware of age-old traditions; her education had set her apart from the simple fisherfolk of her village, yet she had an ingrained peasant's respect for the authority of age, and especially for that of older men. She had evidently made an unsuccessful attempt to reason with her people earlier; her tear-swollen eyes explained why she hesitated before mounting that platform. And, too, Mireille might have feared identifying with a foreigner "against" her friends and relatives.

In that suspended period of time, while Mireille held herself back, Terry's mind weighed several trite and obvious sentences that might encourage the girl. Tell her again that she had to do this for Armand's sake? Mireille knew this. Nor did any stranger have to remind her what the results of total panic might be. Yet she was looking at the health officer's extended hand as though he were coaxing her into a torture chamber. Terry's own hand moved upward impulsively. Without saying a word, she touched the veil of Mireille's nurse's cap. The girl's eyes locked with Terry's for a split second, misting over with tears, yet responding clearly to a message that no one else present could have understood. Then, lifting her chin in a sudden, defiant motion, Mireille let herself be helped up to the bandstand.

She spoke faintly, at first, her voice as deceptively fragile as her small body. *"Il n'y a rien à craindre!"* There was a restless stirring among the people listening to her, and Mireille repeated the phrase more emphatically: *"Il n'y a rien à craindre!"* She glanced down at Terry, inviting the confirmation of — not a mere stranger, but another nurse. "Is true, yes? Nothing is . . . to fear?"

Terry smiled, nodding her head vigorously, conscious that she was being scrutinized carefully, though without resentment.

"Le médecin americain ne part pas," Mireille continued. She spoke more strongly now. *"Croyez-moi! Faites-lui confiance!"*

Terry understood enough to know that the nurse was asking her friends to trust Bill Lindley. The American doctor was not leaving; that was the importance of the message. There seemed to be a general, lingering skepticism, with people looking around them as though the doctor's physical absence made Mireille's words suspect. Mireille must have caught this flaw in her argument; for a moment she looked as though she might give up.

"Doctor Lindley has gone to the clinic in Roberval," Terry called out. To strengthen that fact, she added a slightly less honest embellishment. "He's . . . interested in Dr. Gautier's treatment of the smallpox patient."

Mireille seized upon the casual-sounding and reassuring statement, translating it with inflections that implied, "There, you see? The doctors are not concerned. They are going about their work, while we behave like ninnies."

There were a few sheepish smiles in the crowd, now, and a few attempts at nonchalance. One elderly woman shrugged, looking at the friends around her as though they had behaved rather foolishly, while she had known right along that there was no reason to be concerned.

Encouraged, Mireille cried out, *"Ayez confiance en notre médecin!"*

The plea to put their faith in their own doctor stirred the nationalistic pride of one young fisherman, *"Un médecin français!"*

"Oui Un médecin français!" The echo came from Jean-Pierre. If the villagers were going to place their faith in any doctor, it was going to be their own *French* doctor. Furthermore, the old gardener, having been the unrecognized star of this entire episode, could see no reason why a mere snip of a girl should be the center of attraction. Usually a quiet, even a morose individual, he had been sparked into animation, and with the help of several cronies he was scrambling up to the platform from which he had demonstrated his tone-deafness the night before.

Mireille, pleased to be taken out of the limelight, stepped back. The public health officer looked on with mixed annoyance and relief. And Jean-Pierre, father of two heroic sons as well as the prime authority on those incomprehensible foreigners who inhabited the clifftop villa, raised his hands above his head like a campaigning politician acknowledging the applause of partisans.

His speech was wholly unintelligible to Terry, but the old man's moment of glory was amply illustrated with gestures. At one point, obviously explaining how the foolish Americans had misunderstood his perfectly sensible report, he did a brief pantomime in which Tick Olner's foppish mannerisms were easily recognizable. His audience tittered. Cautiously, a few people glanced at Terry to see if she had been insulted. When they saw that she shared their amusement, their appreciation became bolder, and this was all Jean-Pierre needed. The latent ham in him came forth with an exaggerated imitation of Wanda Olner, complete with the latter's hip-swinging, theatrical walk. The villagers roared. Incredibly, the "bubonic plague" scare had been replaced by an impromptu vaudeville act. Grateful for the chance to escape, Mireille let herself down from the back of the platform.

Terry slipped away from the gathering and joined the French nurse, squeezing Mireille's hand to congratulate her. "You couldn't have done better. Dr. Gautier is going to be terribly proud of you."

Mireille's eyes widened in shock. "I was . . . so *terribly?*"

Terry laughed. "You see how easy it is for us to misunderstand each other? No — you did beautifully, Mireille. The question is, what do we do now?"

"I think . . . to telephone *le docteur* Gautier, *non?*"

"Fine," Terry said. "I imagine he'll advise you to go home and get some rest."

"C'est impossible," the girl protested. "Now we . . . how you say? Is only to begin."

Mireille's prediction was correct. Sensibly, knowing the importance of Jean-Pierre's effect upon the villagers, the public health official let the old gardener's entertainment run its course. Then, before the crowd dispersed, he made a brief speech, asking all of St. Juste's citizens to report to the schoolhouse, where a Red Cross unit was setting up facilities for mass smallpox vaccinations. It was merely a sensible precaution, he emphasized. The intelligent people of St. Juste were certainly not going to ignore the good advice of their own doctor. . . .

Before reporting to the school, Terry took time out to contact Bill Lindley at the clinic, phoning him from the café. She gave him only a brief report on what had transpired, but she made it a point to laud Mireille's role in the proceedings. "Please be sure Armand knows what she did, Bill. She was scared stiff, but she came on like a modern day Joan of Arc."

Bill's quick laugh was reassuring. "I have a feeling I'm being used in a promotional scheme," he said. "It's all right. Gautier's in a good mood."

"What's happening there?"

"I'm doing scut work," Bill said. "I can't practice medicine here, but I've been okayed to unpack supplies. If Gautier doesn't fall on his face from exhaustion first, we'll have everybody in Roberval revaccinated by . . . maybe midnight."

"No mobs burning down the clinic?"

"Don't laugh," Bill cautioned. "When I got here, there were a few jittery characters demanding that Gautier get his smallpox patient out of the town. I guess seeing me convinced them that they'd bought a silly rumor. I used a lot of psychology and my fractured French. You know . . . appeal to civil pride. Nobody in a sophisticated metropolis like Roberval wants to behave like a hayseed from St. Juste. Excuse me a minute."

Bill turned from the telephone, spoke to someone else, then said, "I have to get back to work. I offered to help wherever I could, and Gautier's so pressed, he's taking me at my word. You're going to help there, are you?"

"If they want me," Terry said.

She attributed Bill's final remark to tiredness. "Who wouldn't want you?"

It had been a meaningless, offhand remark — a compliment to her value as a nurse. Yet the words ran through Terry's mind, repeating themselves endlessly throughout the long afternoon and evening as she gave volunteer assistance to the public health team. She was still relishing Bill's words when he came for her, not at midnight, but shortly after nine that evening. Drooping with fatigue, he made an incongruous entrance into the village schoolhouse, carrying a monstrous bouquet of pink roses in his arms.

"This isn't for you," Bill sighed. "I'm just a delivery boy for a busy doctor." Grinning, he handed the flowers to Mireille. "Compliments of Simon Legree. For services above and beyond the call of duty."

Exhausted as she was, Mireille would have staggered under a lesser weight. "Is from . . . a Monsieur Legree? I not think I know. . . ."

"Dr. Gautier. I think the card's signed 'Armand,' " Bill told her. He released a long sigh of wonderment. "I can understand how

France was able to produce famous physicians like Paré, Bernard, and Laënnec without losing its reputation as a country of fabulous lovers." Addressing Terry, he said, "Here's a guy who hasn't closed his eyes in twenty-four hours. He has twenty-six extra hospitalized patients, in addition to his regular case load, including a critical small-pox victim. He quells a near riot and supervises a mass vaccination program in his spare time. And in the midst of all that, he orders roses and sits down to write a flowery note."

Terry shot him a questioning glance. "How do you know it was a flowery note?"

"I was looking at Gautier's face when he wrote it," Bill said. He took Terry's arm and guided her toward the schoolroom door. Mireille was reading the card that had accompanied the roses and took no notice of their leaving. "If you've still got doubts, look back at Mireille while she reads it."

Terry didn't look back. She let Bill lead her out into the star-studded night.

CHAPTER 13

"We got as far as that little bridge where you turn on the main drag," Irene said. She slammed her suitcase shut and sank her full weight on the bed beside it. "Junior gave them quarantine guys a lotta lip. Wanda threw a tantrum, an' Mr. O. tried to give the cop a fistfulla money, but they wasn't buyin' any kinda persuadin'. Real nice an' polite they said to get back here, an' back here we come. Everybody mad at everybody else, except me an' Carl. Heck, we was with a carnival once where half the operators come down with measles. All we did, we sat tight and done what the medics tole us. Like I said to Mr. O., no sense actin' like some kinda nut."

"But you stayed with him," Terry said.

"Sure we did. He ain't got nobody but me an' Carl." Irene kicked off her shoes and exhaled a loud puffing sigh. "Boy, what a day! Even after we got back here, them two brats was talkin' about sneakin' outta here at night . . . like there was some way to get out. By that time, Mr. O. realized the whole thing was stupid, and them two . . . they got so nasty, I finally let 'em have it. I mean, I really tole 'em what I thought. I felt sorry I did that, on accounta it prob'ly hurt the boss to hear the truth. The thing is, though, he didn't come out an' disagree with me. He just went in his room, lookin' real sad."

"I wonder if I should go and talk to him?" Terry asked. "I've got all my things packed. I guess I'll be leaving in the morning."

"I wouldn't go in there," Irene advised. "The doc's talkin' to him now, an' Mr. O. prob'ly feels cheap enough around him. If you was to go in there . . . I dunno. The best thing you can do is not embarrass him, kid. All he wants to do is go back home an' forget the whole thing."

Terry weighed the advice in her mind for a few minutes and then decided to accept it. A confrontation with Richard could only humiliate him. Completely alone now, except for the Washburns, he would cherish more than ever the dearest of his possessions — his pride.

Carl came into the garage apartment shortly afterward, and Terry chatted with him and with Irene briefly, reviewing the past crowded hours and then exchanging goodbyes with the couple. Afterward, reluctant to go into the main house before she was certain that the Olners were asleep, she walked onto the terrace, sinking into one of the lounge chairs.

In spite of the unpleasantness she had encountered here at the villa, she felt a deep melancholy that was entirely separate from her weariness. She had looked forward to seeing the Riviera, enjoying the fabulous resort centers down the coast from St. Juste, the flower-growing perfume center of Grasse, the excitement promised in travel circulars describing the glamorous azure coast. And tomorrow she would be leaving this house; the day after that she would be boarding a plane, going back home, perhaps never to see these promised wonders at all. Bill would remain. There were still several weeks left of his vacation; he would not spend them alone. If she could have seen the Riviera with Bill . . .

"I was afraid you'd gone to sleep," Terry heard him say.

For a few seconds she was not certain whether Bill's quiet appearance was genuine, or only part and parcel of her wistful daydream. It was real enough. He started to pull up another of the lounge chairs, then changed his mind and said, "We're right under everybody's bedroom window here. Would you still have the energy for a short walk?"

He thrust out his hand and Terry grasped it, letting Bill pull her to her feet. "I have a lot to say," he told her. "I'd just as soon say it without an audience."

They reached the stone wall from which, on other occasions, Terry had looked out to sea alone. She was too dazed by the suddenness of Bill's presence to wonder why he didn't want to be overheard. But her heart had commenced a nearly audible thumping. She perched herself on the wall, stunned by Bill's position. He stood before her like an angry schoolteacher facing an unruly classroom.

"Why didn't you tell me you weren't going to marry Richard?" Bill demanded. "Why do I have to get all my information about you second hand? From Gautier this afternoon, from Richard just now . . . ?"

"I didn't tell you because . . ." Terry gasped. "It wasn't necessary to tell anyone. It never occurred to me!"

Bill laughed suddenly, reaching down to sweep Terry into his arms. "I'm not reading the riot act to you, darling. I'm calling myself an idiot." He pressed his lips against

Terry's, gently at first and then, as she responded, lifted his face from hers, placed her arms around his neck, and kissed her again. This time there was a hunger in his kiss that spoke more clearly than words. (Unbelievable . . . she was dreaming. . . . She would open her eyes and he would be gone. . . . It was impossible!)

It had happened. Bill was holding her close, understanding the reason for her tears better than Terry herself understood. "Are you upset because of what Gautier told me, darling? That you're in love with me? I would have discovered that for myself. This morning, when Richard gave up his right to . . ."

"He never had any right!" Terry cried.

"I should have realized that, too, knowing Richard. But he was so matter of fact, so positive! I don't think he was home from the hospital two weeks, before he told me you were going to be the next Mrs. Olner. I was sick about it, but I congratulated him. In the past, whenever he said he was going to do something, the word was as good as the deed." Bill tightened his arms around Terry, as though remembering that their near loss of each other was still a threat. "When you decided to take this vacation with him, I knew it had to be true.

"I didn't know whether I was booking passage to be near you or . . . just to torture myself — seeing the two of you together."

"Is that why you ignored me completely? Why you . . . let me eat my heart out with jealousy?"

"I had to lose myself somehow, Terry. I figured . . . Wanda and Tick couldn't have hated you so thoroughly unless you were a genuine threat to their inheritance. Richard had them convinced, too. This whole trip was a maneuver to weld all of you into one big happy family."

"He's a . . . very convincing salesman," Terry said quietly. "The only person he never sold was . . ."

"You. And I'd be feeling sorry for him right now, if I thought it was possible for Richard to have his heart broken." Bill kissed Terry's forehead. "He's a little depressed right now, but no more so than once when a merger he'd counted on fell through. Defeat is an inspiration to him. It gives him purpose. Tomorrow he'll tackle a bigger project."

"Bill?"

"Yes?"

"I don't want to talk about Richard. I know all I want to know about the Olners.

And I . . . I know so little about you, except that . . ."

"Except . . . ?"

". . . that I love you, Bill. I've loved you for a long time." Terry turned her face upward, looking into Bill's eyes and seeing for the first time that the miracle was not a product of her imagination. Even here, in the semi-darkness, what she saw there could not be mistaken for anything but love. "Not that anything else really matters. But I want to know all about you. Your hopes, your dreams . . ."

Bill hugged her closer and released a quick laugh of pure joy. "My hope is . . . that we can get out of here early enough tomorrow morning to find somebody to marry us before we take off for Nice. I think it would be reassuring to have a marriage license before we leave on our honeymoon. Right?"

"Bill . . ."

"Don't interrupt. You asked me, remember? Okay. Hope number two. That Gautier and that nurse he's suddenly become aware of can spare whatever time it takes to serve as witnesses. He's already agreed to give freely of his copious free time."

"You talked to Armand about . . . witnessing our wedding?"

"Now you're making me sound as presumptuous as Richard," Bill protested. "I didn't take you for granted, Terry. The offer was made and I accepted it . . . tentatively. What else did you want to know about me? My dreams."

There was a long, fulfilling silence while Bill pressed his lips hard against Terry's, and while she wondered again if this unbelievably balmy night and this unbelievably beautiful place was an illusion that would melt away — that none of this would be real; Bill's arms around her, the warmth of him, the incredible things she had heard him say . . .

"Dreams," Bill said after a long while. He said it with mock thoughtfulness, as though he were trying to recall some memorable dream out of a far-distant past. "I think this one will do for the present, darling. I'm assuming there'll be others . . . tomorrow . . . next week . . . for the rest of our lives. Right now, I'll settle for this one. Any more questions?"

Terry closed her eyes and let Bill draw her closer. "No more questions," she whispered. "No more questions at all."

We hope you have enjoyed this Large Print book. Other Thorndike and Wheeler Large Print books are available at your library or directly from the publishers.

For information about titles and ordering please call or write without obligation to:

Publisher
Thorndike Press
295 Kennedy Memorial Drive
Waterville, ME 04901 USA
Tel. (800) 223-1244

or visit our Web site at:

www.gale.com/thorndike
www.gale.com/wheeler

OR

Chivers Large Print
published by BBC Audiobooks Ltd
St James House, The Square
Lower Bristol Road
Bath BA2 3SB
England
Tel. +44(0) 800 136919
email: bigprint@bbc.co.uk
www.bbcaudiobooks.co.uk

All our Large Print titles are designed for easy reading, and all our books are made to last.